"We're consenting adults."

Her eyes closed as she came up on tiptoe and parted her swollen lips.

His heart-rate skyrocketed and his hands went to her bare shoulders, pushing her firmly back down on her heels. "You don't mean that."

"Well, we *are*," she pouted.

"I mean you don't mean that the way it sounded."

She paused, eyebrows going up, jewel eyes shimmering expectantly. "How—exactly—did it sound?"

He stared at her, hard. "Like you want to go to bed with me."

Dear Reader

When my wonderful friend Colleen Collins and I finished writing our connected Mills & Boon® Sensual Romances™, TOO CLOSE TO CALL and TOO CLOSE FOR COMFORT, we knew we had to do it again right away. We crafted the perfect boyfriend list and realised we were on to something fun!

Colleen picked a sports bar setting for her story, and I just knew I had to find a sexy athlete for Megan. Irish soccer player Collin O'Patrick is the perfect match. He's famous, but down-to-earth, and ready to defend his sport to the end. When Megan insults professional athletes on her radio show, Collin steps up to the plate to defend them. He takes Megan on over the airwaves, and the result is a sizzling banter that sends the ratings through the roof.

I hope you enjoy THE PERFECT BOYFRIEND. And be sure to look for THE PERFECT GIRLFRIEND, by Colleen Collins, to read about Cecily's romance.

I love hearing from readers. Please feel free to drop me a line through my website at barbaradunlop.com

Happy reading!

Barbara Dunlop

Recent titles by the same author:

HIGH STAKES
FLYING HIGH

THE PERFECT BOYFRIEND

BY
BARBARA DUNLOP

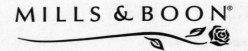

MILLS & BOON®

First published in Great Britain 2006
Harlequin Mills & Boon Limited,
Eton House, 18-24 Paradise Road, Richmond, Surrey TW9 1SR

© Barbara Dunlop 2006

ISBN 0 263 84989 9

Set in Times Roman 10½ on 13¼ pt.
171-0506-45193

Printed and bound in Spain
by Litografia Rosés S.A., Barcelona

For my husband
The Perfect Boyfriend

PROLOGUE

"How much does it cost to hire a hit man?" Megan Brock slammed the door of her best friend's apartment shut behind her.

Cecily Cassell glanced up, her eyes widening to saucer size as she lifted her foot from the pedal of her industrial sewing machine. The whirring motor went silent. "What in the *hell* are you wearing?"

"A leather bra," said Megan, striding her way across Cecily's living room.

Cecily's gaze traveled up and down Megan's body. She gestured with her hand as the pitch of her voice went higher. "And…and…"

"And a matching skirt." Megan paused. "You think I can find one on the Internet?"

"A leather skirt?"

"A hit man."

"Oh."

Megan hit the power button on the computer. "Do you have any idea what that son of a bitch did?"

Cecily shook her head. "I could not begin to guess."

"He told me I was repressed." Megan stabbed her thumb against her chest. "Me! You think I'm repressed?"

She didn't wait for Cecily's answer.

"Apparently, I haven't been making enough noise during sex." She punched the keyboard with her fingertip, launching the Internet browser. "Funny, I didn't know there was a quota."

Cecily opened her mouth, but Megan kept on talking. "He says I'm repressed. Says I should let loose. Says he wants to see me in a leather skirt."

"Wow," said Cecily, her eyes growing wider by the second.

"And I'm thinking, okay, maybe we aren't talking head-banging and fireworks. Maybe it's partly my fault. Hey, who knows better than me that it's all in the packaging? I work in advertising. If a leather skirt's going to do it for him, where's the harm?"

She typed in the words "hit man" and clicked search. "You think they'll take American Express?"

"Everybody takes American Express." Cecily pushed her chair away from the dining table, arranging the pile of pinstriped fabric beside the machine.

"Good point."

Cecily tapped her way across the hardwood floor to the tiny kitchenette, calling over her shoulder. "Keep talking."

Megan scrolled down the list of web sites on the computer screen. "So, *un*repressed, fun-loving, easy-going woman that I am, I put on the skirt. And, I'll admit it, it felt kind of sexy. But then he pulls out the freakin' bra." She turned to face Cecily, gesturing to her black-leather-clad breasts. "I'm not as crazy about the bra. I mean, it makes me look like a biker chick at Daytona, don't you think?"

Cecily cocked her head to one side as she pulled a tray of ice cubes out of her frost-laden freezer. "It's the studded choker that makes the biggest impact on me."

"I should have clued in." Megan reached for the back of her neck, ripping at the buckle on the stupid choker. She glanced at the computer screen. So far the words "hit man" had found her a fishing charter service, several police blotters, an article in *Texas Monthly* and a cricket champion out of London. "You think the FBI tracks this stuff?"

"Leather clothing?"

"Internet searches."

"I think that's the CIA."

"Oh. And they're probably more interested in international terrorists than one-off killers like me, right?"

Cecily dumped the ice cubes into her blender. "Probably. So, what was it you should have clued into?"

"That he was a sicko freak. I'm all dressed up, thinking, okay, this isn't doing it for me, but I'll parade around the apartment for a few minutes. Then he says he wants to go for a drive. I say, uh-uh, no way, you are *not* getting me out in public."

Megan paced across the room. "But then he starts begging and whining, and sending me on a guilt trip. He gives me an overcoat, and promises we'll go out the back stairs to the underground parking. Just for a little drive in the city lights. I look so beautiful, so sexy, so hot, he can hardly stand it."

Cecily added a measure of tequila.

"*Un*repressed." Megan's voice rose with the memory. "Did I mention I was *un*repressed?"

"Yes, you did," said Cecily.

"We get in the car. I turf the coat in the back seat. By now, I'm not feeling sexy at all. I'm feeling cheap and sleazy."

Cecily dumped in another glug of tequila.

"We head across town and stop in front of this boarded-up storefront. He tells me it's a nightclub. He tells me I'm in for the time of my life. His eyes light up—I swear to God they were glowing—he tells me he's going to teach me the meaning of the word 'respect'."

Cecily upended the bottle. "You think one lime's enough?"

"One lime sounds about perfect to me." A fresh spurt of anger tore through Megan. If she ever saw the man again…

"So, what did you do?" asked Cecily.

"Since the angle wasn't right to emasculate him with a well-placed stiletto, I walked out."

"Looking like *that*?"

"Got a taxi quick enough, and several lucrative offers while I waited on the curb." She nodded at the blender. "You gonna make those drinks?"

"Absolutely." Cecily hit a button and the clatter of ice filled the apartment.

Megan headed for the bedroom, snapping the bra

open, kicking off her high heels and shimmying out of the tight skirt.

For three months she'd dated the creep, always understanding when he was short on cash and she had to pick up the check, forgiving him when he was late because his buddies begged him to stay for another beer, breathing shallow when his aftershave turned on him, and generally trying like hell to make the relationship work.

At twenty-five, her biological clock wasn't exactly ticking into overtime, but she'd always assumed she'd meet the right man after college. Now she was three years out of her advertising degree and working hard to establish her own agency—without a decent relationship in sight.

Were there *no* Prince Charmings out there?

She commandeered a pair of Cecily's faded sweatpants and a stained, oversized Broncos T-shirt.

When she got back to the living room, Cecily was pouring the margaritas.

Megan flopped down on the couch, curling her bare feet beneath her and sighed hard. "Next man I date is going to *love* me in sweatpants."

Cecily handed her a tall, frosty drink. "Next man I date is going to own a Lear jet."

"Laugh at my jokes," said Megan, taking a long, satisfying sip.

Cecily took the other end of the couch. "Bring me flowers."

"Have an Australian accent."

"You like Australian accents?"

"They're sexy."

Cecily took a drink, affecting a pretty good drawl. "I'm gonna teach ya the meanin' of respect, Sheila."

Megan laughed. "See, when you say it in Australian, it almost sounds sexy."

Cecily shook her head. "I can't believe he said that."

"I can't believe he lived."

Cecily raised her glass in a toast. "My next boyfriend is going to make blender drinks."

"Open doors," said Megan.

"Always pay."

"Love my mother, my senile grandmother and my slobbery dog."

"You don't have a slobbery dog."

Megan shrugged. "If I had one, he'd love it."

"We should be writing these down," said Cecily.

"Excellent idea." Megan clambered off the couch and went for the telephone desk, grabbing a notebook and pen. "It'll give us a frame of reference for our next dates." She polished off the last of her drink. "We might not always have this clarity of thought."

"There's more in the blender," said Cecily.

Megan dropped the pen and paper in Cecily's lap on her way by. "Don't forget licensed masseuse."

Cecily started to write. "And he's interested in my career."

Megan topped up both of their glasses with the blender pitcher. "Now *this* is something that deserves to be on the Internet. I bet there are hundreds of women out there who could benefit from our list."

CHAPTER ONE

MEGAN considered that in the karma cycle of her life, there were good ideas, bad ideas and five-martini ideas. Fortunately, she hadn't had many five-martini ideas. Or at least none that she had acted on.

*Un*fortunately, this one had slipped through the cracks. Though she supposed, technically, it was a five-margarita idea. But, as the public service spots so deftly pointed out, all drinks were equal when they hit your bloodstream, or was that your brain?

She stared at the black microphone on the table in front of her and tried to work up a little saliva in her paper-dry mouth. It had seemed like such a *good* idea during that margarita haze of three months ago—posting the "perfect boyfriend" list to the Internet, helping other women who were having trouble with their relationships.

And it had worked.

She and Cecily had received fifty e-mails the first day, hundreds the first week. Eventually, a small publisher had asked them to write a book—an offer they'd happily accepted, knowing it was an opportunity to reach even more women in need. But now they were guests on a local radio talk show, and Megan couldn't stop thinking of the hundreds, no, *thousands* of people sitting by their radios, about to listen to her make a fool of herself.

It was one thing to respond to people in writing, when she had time to think about her answer, collaborate with Cecily, frame it, craft it correctly. But on live radio? Talk about a chance to make a fool of herself. Or, worse, talk about a chance to give out stupid advice that screwed up somebody's life.

Seriously screwed it up.

Maybe permanently screwed it up.

She glanced at Cecily for support, and Cecily smiled nervously back.

Behind a sheet of glass, the sound technician adjusted dials and slide switches in the control room. Sherri Rodney, the radio host, shuffled papers while she talked into her microphone to an unseen producer whose voice was coming through one side of Megan's headphones.

"Thirty seconds," came the man's voice.

Sherri adjusted her microphone, squaring the pile of papers in front of her as the music faded away. "That was 'Long Hot Summer' by The Candidates. And I hope you've got your air-conditioning turned on out there, Denver, because we've got something hot coming up for you. This is Sherri Rodney on KNOA radio forty-five, coming to you live from downtown Denver."

Megan swallowed, straightening in her chair. Her

heart rate started to climb, and she rubbed her sweaty palms across her old jeans. She was dying to take another sip of water, but she was starting to worry about her bladder holding out for the entire hour.

If she were a better person, now would be the time to swear off margaritas.

"Any of you women out there recovering from a bad breakup?" asked Sherri. "Anybody using their ex's picture as a dartboard? Anybody got his number on speed dial so you can practice all those four-letter words your mother warned you not to use?

"If you answered yes to any of those questions, do *we* have the guests for *you*."

Sherri gave both Megan and Cecily encouraging smiles. "With me in the studio this evening are Megan Brock and Cecily Cassell, authors of the original Internet list, and the cult phenomenon handbook, *The Perfect Boyfriend*. Welcome to the show, ladies."

"Thank you," Megan rasped through reluctant vocal cords. She swallowed against her parched throat, pulse leaping with her growing panic. How was she going to get through a radio show without a voice?

"Thank you," Cecily echoed from the opposite side of the octagonal table. Her face was partially obscured by the overhead mike stand, and Megan shifted so she could take courage from Cecily's eyes.

"Let's start with you, Megan," said Sherri. "I understand this rise to fame started with a list the two of you posted to the Internet on how to be the perfect boyfriend. What was the inspiration?"

"The inspiration?" asked Megan, not quite understanding the question.

"What made you decide to write the list?"

Megan's eyes widened as her mind flashed back to the sleazy S and M club. No way in the world was she about to tell a million Denver listeners about her black leather push-up bra and the studded collar. But she couldn't for the life of her think up a lie.

As Sherri made a frantic motion with her hand Megan's stomach bottomed out, her gaze flying back to Cecily in a panic.

"In my case," Cecily inserted, voice quavering only slightly, "I foolishly followed a guy from West L.A. to Denver. Gave up my job, my apartment. Paid to move his sorry-ass, faded puce couch halfway across the country, and then he turns into the boyfriend from hell." Cecily paused. "Am I allowed to say hell on the air?"

"Yes." Sherri winked, grinning broadly. "But I'm going to have to ask you not to say ass."

"Too bad," said Megan. "Because she kicked his sorry ass out on the street." Too late, she remembered her microphone.

Luckily, Sherri and Cecily both laughed.

"Looks like we have our first caller," said Sherri. "Roxy from Aurora. Go ahead, Roxy."

"My last boyfriend?" said Roxy, in a slightly nasal voice. "Dumped me on February thirteenth! February fifteenth, he calls wantin' some sugar. I told him, no way, sucker. We broke up. Then he tells me he *always* breaks up with his girlfriend before Valentine's Day, so he doesn't have to cough up for a gift."

"Ever heard of that before?" asked Sherri, eyebrows going up.

"Oh, yeah," said Megan, nodding. She'd heard that and much worse over the past few months. "Believe it or not, it happens every holiday. That's the reason we wrote chapter four. It's called Chucking the Cheap Date. Trust me, you want to chuck those guys far and fast."

"Oh, I chucked him all right," said Roxy. "Guy wants me on his arm, he comes through with the goods."

Megan caught Cecily's eye. They both smiled at Roxy's self-assurance. The world needed more women like her.

"For any of you male listeners out there?" Megan put in. "Looking to keep a fine woman like Roxy? Eat the candy, give the flowers to your mother, and head for the nearest jewelry store for a gift worth wrapping."

"Amen," said Roxy.

"Thanks for calling," said Sherri. "Looks like we've got Patty next. Go ahead, Patty."

"Do guys not have a *clue*?" asked Patty.

Megan paused, waiting to see if Cecily wanted to take this one. She didn't speak up, so Megan went for it. Amazingly, she was starting to have fun.

"Not even a whiff of a clue," she said to the caller.

"I once dated a guy who made me split a ten-dollar check," complained Patty. "What the hell is that about?"

"*That* is a man so cheap his ba—" Megan cleared her throat. "His knees squeak. Chapter ten: If He Doesn't Pay, He Doesn't Stay."

"On our next date—"

"There was a *next* date?" asked Megan in amazement. "I think we'd better send in some professional help, Patty."

"That's why I bought your book. Second date he ogles a set of knockers in a red tube top, then asks me if it bothers me much, having such small breasts."

Megan gasped.

Patty snorted. "Got my brewski in the lap for his trouble."

"Hope it was on his tab," said Megan.

"It was."

"Right on," exclaimed Cecily.

"Right on," Megan echoed.

"Right on," said Sherri, holding back a laugh. "It appears there are a lot of dissatisfied women out there."

"If by dissatisfied women," said Megan, "you mean a lot of loser men? Then, you're right."

"And how do you expect the list and the book to help?" asked Sherri.

"It's all about empowerment." Megan, warming to the topic, looked to Cecily for confirmation.

Cecily nodded.

"If we can demonstrate to women that they deserve respect, consideration and attention," Megan continued, "they're going to feel empowered enough to ask for it. At the same time, if we can hold an unflinching mirror up to the men of this country, they're going to realize their behavior is unacceptable. Breaking up for Valentine's Day? Come on. That's inexcusable." She took a breath. "I bet Roxy had a gift ready for him."

"And now we have Carmen on line three," said Sherri. "Go ahead, Carmen."

Turned out, Carmen's boyfriend spent all his money on *Star Wars* paraphernalia. Then Edith's husband had an affair with a younger woman. Then Wendy's date asked for a threesome with her sister. And Juanita's boyfriend dropped off his dirty laundry every Monday night.

It was clear to Megan that all of those men were worthless, and she said so. After some discussion, the callers agreed, impressing Megan with their intelligence and their sense of humor.

She felt as if they'd just gotten started, when the music came up and Sherri said, "Thank you for your calls, Denver. And thanks for joining us here on KNOA radio forty-five." The music came up, and the lights on the microphones went out.

Megan was still jazzed, waiting to talk to the next caller.

Cecily stripped off her headphones and rounded the table to give Megan a hug. "You were *great!*"

"So were you."

"I barely said anything."

Megan suddenly realized Cecily was right. Her smile disappeared. "Oh. I'm sorry." She'd been having so much fun laughing and commiserating with the callers, she hadn't even realized she'd monopolized the conversation.

Cecily shook her head. "Oh, no, you don't. You were a hit."

A big, balding man suddenly flung open the door and burst into the booth. "Roland Scavolini," he boomed, striding across the small room, hand held out in greeting. "The producer of the show. How would you ladies like to come back?"

Megan stopped midshake, looking at Cecily, who blinked in surprise.

Roland shook his head, his grin widening. "We had callers lighting up the entire switchboard. I know a hit when I see one."

Megan was game to do it again. People were obviously relating the stories to their own lives. If tonight's callers were anything to go by, there was a lot of work to be done in the greater Denver area.

Maybe she and Cecily could start a dating revolution! She raised her eyebrows in Cecily's direction.

Cecily looked a little less certain.

"I'm prepared to offer you a contract here and now," said Roland.

"A contract?" Cecily perked up. "As in money?"

Cecily's fashion-design business was in serious need of cash. Not that Megan's advertising agency was in such terrific shape. Just this morning, she'd spent several hours going over the books, trying to juggle accounts payable, overdue receivables, payroll and utilities. Clients were slow in coming and sometimes slower to pay.

Roland nodded.

"How much?" Cecily asked.

He named a very respectable sum.

Cecily's eyes narrowed. "Throw in two minutes of ad time, and you've got yourself a deal."

He hesitated. "What are you going to advertise?"

"My fashion-design business, Well Suited, and Megan's ad agency, Point To Point."

"We're back on in twenty seconds," said Sherri.

"Deal," said Roland.

Cecily grinned, and Megan felt a rush of excitement at the thought of bringing their Perfect Boyfriend advice to thousands more people.

Roland turned to Sherri. "Plug the new show. It'll air Tuesday nights at nine. Call it 'The Perfect Boyfriend'."

Collin O'Patrick stripped off his sweaty soccer jersey as he headed through the locker-room door at Invesco Field, wadding it up in a ball and tossing it into the laundry bag. There was definitely a long, hot-tub soak with his name on it tonight.

He'd had a great game. Brett Stirling had fed him a sweetheart of a pass at halftime for the tying goal, then he'd managed to redirect a shot from Griffin, catching the goalie off guard for the go-ahead at minute sixty-seven. The team was coming together as they headed into mid season, and it felt like poetry in motion.

"Sweet goal, O'Patrick." Brett slapped him on the shoulder. The noise level in the locker room rose as fifteen players, the coach, the manager, and support staff all piled in, exuberant over the win.

"Better than sex," Collin said to Brett as he opened his locker.

"Debatable," said Brett, stretching his own jersey over his head and pulling out the elastic that held back his dark shoulder-length hair. "Coming with us to Home Plate tonight?"

Collin shook his head, pushing his sweaty, short hair back from his forehead. He sat down on the bench to remove his cleats. "Put myself out there to be stared at by loyal fans and accosted by sports reporters? No, thanks. My ego can stand on its own two feet."

"Don't be so hasty. Some of those fans are blonde. You could test out the 'scoring goals versus having sex' theory. Personally, I'm putting fifty bucks on sex."

"Don't you ever get tired of the circus?" asked Collin.

Brett did it all—personal appearances, sports-drink ads, autographs and brand-name clothes.

"It's not a circus," said Brett. "It's our life."

"It might be your life. But I'm a soccer player, not a billboard."

"Grab the gusto while you can," returned Brett. "Those knees of yours aren't going to last forever."

Collin stripped off his shorts. "My salary's enough."

"It's not like we're in the NBA," said Brett as they ducked their way through the noisy crowd and headed for the showers. "Nobody in North America's earning millions in professional soccer."

"Nice goal, O'Patrick," one of the other players called.

Collin gave him a wave of thanks. "That's because your priorities are screwed up."

"Beer, babes and money?" Brett counted off. "What do you mean screwed up?"

"I mean you colonials have no respect for the game."

"Sure we do," said Brett. "But we also have respect

for the almighty dollar. Stop by for a beer. I'll lie and tell them you're the water boy."

Collin chuckled. His blunt honesty was one of the things he liked about Brett.

"Seriously," argued Brett. "What are you going to do at home? Watch the replays?"

Collin turned on the shower spray, considering that for a moment. What *was* he planning to do at home?

He could always hit the hot tub later. And a beer with the guys didn't sound like such a bad idea. He'd had a great game. Why be in such a hurry to end the night?

He nodded. "Okay. One beer. But don't you go promoting me all over the room again."

"Who me?"

"You think I don't remember that night in Orlando? You were like a used-car salesman on steroids."

Brett grinned. "But she was seriously *hot*."

"She was a soccer groupie."

"And your point is?"

Collin shook his head. "You tell anyone who I am, and you'll be heading balls through your ass."

"I don't think that's anatomically possible."

"Maybe not, but if you screw me on this, we'll find out."

The Home Plate sports bar was crowded and rocking by the time Collin and Brett shouldered their way through the double-glass doorway and into the crowd.

"Collin O'Patrick?" asked an excited voice to Collin's immediate left.

A bunch of heads turned his way.

"Nah," said Brett. "That's the water boy."

"It's Collin O'Patrick," said the affronted young man. He didn't look old enough to be in a bar. "Can I have your autograph, Mr. O'Patrick?"

Collin glared at Brett, who held up his hands in a gesture of innocence. Another fan accosted Brett, holding out the night's program and a pen.

Collin turned back to the young man. He leaned a little closer to talk above the the din of a wide-screen boxing match and dozens of conversations. "You old enough to be in here?"

"Twenty-one today." The young man beamed.

"Happy birthday," said Collin, taking the pen. "What's your name?"

"Michael. Can you sign it to Mike?"

"Sure." Collin scrawled "Happy Birthday, Mike" above his signature.

"Thanks, Mr. O'Patrick," said Mike, in a voice full of awe.

"Call me Collin." He wanted to tell Mike to calm down. He was just a guy who happened to be good at kicking soccer balls. It wasn't as if he was curing cancer.

Mike squared his shoulders, his hero-worship obviously rising to new heights. "Thank you, *Collin*."

"You in college?" asked Collin.

"Yes."

"What's your major?"

"Nutritional science."

"Now *that's* a great profession," said Collin. "You'll help people stay healthy, live longer."

Mike nodded. "Hey, man, if you ever have any questions—"

"Collin?" Brett pushed against Collin's shoulder, steering him into the crowd.

"Sorry, Mike," said Collin. "Looks like I gotta go."

"You sign the autograph," Brett instructed as they wove their way through the crowded tables. "You don't become their best friend. No wonder you suck at this."

"I was just trying to make the poor kid relax."

"He doesn't want to relax. He wants to believe you're a god."

"Right," Collin scoffed. "Like I'm so much more deserving than Nobel Peace Prize winners."

"Nobel Peace Prize winners don't score goals against Carlos Cabella."

"Hey, O'Patrick, Stirling." One of the players waved them over to a big, crowded table.

Collin slipped onto the bench seat next to his coach. He accepted a beer from the waitress, but when he tried to pay her she told him the beer was complimentary for soccer stars. Then she asked him to sign a napkin for her nephew.

He signed the napkin and gave her the five as a tip.

"Listen to this," somebody shouted from the bar. A man reached up and cranked the volume on a sound system.

"Professional athletes are the *worst* offenders," came a woman's smooth voice.

That snagged Collin's immediate attention. The conversation level dipped and the boxing-match announcer faded into the background.

"Little boys who never really grew up," said the

voice on the radio. "Still battling each other to be king of the sandbox."

The bar crowd booed, and Collin's hand tightened on his beer. Now *that* attitude showed a definite lack of respect for the game.

"It's hard not to pity them," she continued as the conversation in the sports bar faded to nothing. "Not a lot of room for brains amongst all that ego and testosterone. And don't even get me started on unshaven, beer-swilling sports fans who can't pry themselves out of the easy chair with a forklift on Sunday mornings."

"Who *is* that?" asked Collin to the table in general. He might have gone to college on a soccer scholarship, but he'd graduated Magna Cum Laude.

"Megan Brock," said a passing waitress. "Isn't she great?"

Collin gave the woman a perplexed frown.

"I mean," the waitress quickly tried to backpedal as she realized she was standing in a crowd of athletes and sports fans, "I'm *sure* she doesn't mean *you* guys."

"Who does she mean?" asked Collin as Megan Brock's voice droned on with insult after insult.

"You know, uh, fullbacks," said the waitress.

"What's wrong with being a fullback?"

"Collin." Brett's tone was a warning as he gave an almost imperceptible nod in the waitress's direction. "*She's* not the one on the radio."

Collin quickly apologized.

"If you disagree, you can call in," the woman said brightly.

"Call in?"

"It's a phone-in show. 303-555-6213."

Without a word, but with a shit-eating grin on his face, Brett handed Collin a cell phone.

Collin was just angry enough to dial.

The line was busy. He hit redial twenty times. Before he could get through, Megan Brock signed off with a parting shot. "If a professional athlete asks you out, ladies? Do yourself a favor and get his accountant's number instead."

Collin swore.

"You want to rebut?" asked his coach.

"Yes!"

The coach grinned, tucking his own phone back into his suit pocket. "Good. I just talked to the producer. You're booked as a guest next Tuesday."

CHAPTER TWO

WHEN Collin O'Patrick swaggered into the KNOA radio studio on Tuesday night, his short, dark hair curling across his forehead, an overdue shave shadowing his square chin, and the set of his broad shoulders telegraphing the fact that he was ready to rumble, Megan practically swallowed her microphone. She didn't know what she'd been expecting—a fresh-faced beach boy in a numbered jersey? A clean-cut, debonair European? Definitely not those daunting gray eyes, the worn khaki Tee and a pair of blue jeans that bracketed his slim hips like a lover.

She ripped her gaze away from the tell-tale crease across his fly as Cecily inhaled sharply beside her.

"Be still my beating heart," Cecily muttered.

"He's just a man," Megan whispered in return, pulling her unruly hormones up short.

"Yeah. A man I'd like to smoke a cigarette with," said Cecily.

"You quit," said Megan.

"I meant metaphorically."

Metaphorically—Megan might, too. That was if she hadn't learned good looks were a very poor gauge of gray matter. And if her producer hadn't already warned her that Collin was an unreasonable, ego-bound jock.

She took a deep breath, rising to her feet to hold out her hand. "You must be Collin O'Patrick."

He nodded, taking a few long strides toward her. "Megan or Cecily?" His big hand closed around hers. It was cool and dry, exerting enough strength to make the contact meaningful, even while he obviously held his power in check.

Megan tried to keep her hormones from revving up again. "I'm Megan Brock. And this is Cecily Cassell."

One side of his mouth curved up in a mocking half-smile, the flint in his eyes throwing out a definite challenge. "Of course you are. I'd have recognized that rapier voice anywhere."

She let her gaze travel down his worn blue jeans to his scuffed hikers. "Funny. I barely recognized you without your ball."

He cocked his head sideways, the other side of his mouth turning up as the grin became full-fledged. "Oh, I brought my ball all right."

Her eyebrows flexed.

His tone dropped, and his Irish accent became more pronounced. "Figured I'd be needin' both of them, goin' up against you."

Megan felt a shiver of sexual awareness, followed by a quick adrenalin rush as her brain latched on to the challenge of his words. She determinedly put the sexual awareness on hold. "Collin, by the end of the hour, your balls are—"

"Sound check," came the technician's voice over the loudspeaker.

Cecily pointed to a chair for Collin. "Put on the headset," she instructed, sounding as if she was holding back a laugh. "And don't lean into the microphone."

Collin folded his big body into the padded chair, the casters whirring against the plastic mat as he settled into place.

"My balls are what?" he asked into the microphone.

"That's a check on Collin." The sound man's voice was laced with laughter.

Megan hesitated for only a split second. "Mine," she stated crisply as she sat down.

"Check on Megan," the sound man sputtered.

Collin leaned back, lacing his fingers behind his head. "Any time, any place," he drawled.

"Thirty seconds," said the sound technician.

Megan's jaw dropped, and her eyes narrowed at the triumphant expression on Collin's face. "You do realize," she stated, "that this means war."

"I'd be counting on that."

"Just so you two know—" Cecily plunked on her own headset "—I'm staying *way* the hell out of this."

"And that's a check on Cecily."

Megan kept her gaze fixed on Collin as the intro music came up, then faded away.

"Good evening, Denver," Cecily sang cheerfully, not a trace of hesitation in her voice. Over the past few weeks, they'd both grown accustomed to talking on the air.

"It's Tuesday," Megan chimed in as she always did. "And welcome to The Perfect Boyfriend show,"

"As usual," said Cecily, "you can call us at 555-6213 and get your comments and questions on the air. But we also have a special treat tonight. We have a guest here in the studio with us."

Megan took over, smirking into Collin's dark gray eyes as she spoke. "That's right, Denver. Tonight, we're talking with Collin O'Patrick." She paused for a meaningful second. "I know. I can hear you out there, now. *Who?* you're asking." Then she laughed softly. "Well, that's what I asked, too. Turns out Collin O'Patrick is a world-famous soccer player.

"That's right. Here, live, in the KNOA studio, we have a professional athlete ready to explain why he's the perfect boyfriend. I'm told Collin took exception to our show last week. And, well, since we're always open to a good debate here at The Perfect Boyfriend, we invited him to join us.

"First, let me say, welcome, Collin." She laced the words with syrupy sweetness.

Collin gave her a mocking smile. "Why, thank you, Megan. Delighted to be here."

"Tell us, Collin," said Cecily, "while we wait for the phones to light up, what qualifies you as the perfect boyfriend?"

"Well, Cecily, since I never actually claimed to *be* the perfect boyfriend, I think the important question is, why have you two set yourselves up as the barometer of perfection?"

Megan jumped in. "Nice try." She acknowledged his attempt to turn the tables. "But it's not just *our* barometer. We have thousands of letters and testimonials from women supporting our list."

"And I have thousands of letters from women offering me everything from homemade pies to sex to becoming the mother of my children," said Collin. "And not a single one of them seemed to give a rat's patoot whether or not I—" he held up his fingers to count off the list "—shaved frequently, made blender drinks or talked about my feelings."

Megan settled into the rhythm of the debate, her brain starting to hum. "Are you saying because some sports groupies are willing to throw themselves at you, sight unseen, that the women of the world should settle for an unkempt, conceited boor who is totally focused on his ego and his teammates—?"

"Are you saying men should conform to a silly, superficial list which not only emasculates—?"

Megan shifted forward. "There's nothing silly or superficial about a man who is a good listener and is interested in my career."

"If he's *always doing it your way*, he's a lapdog, not a man."

"Time for our first caller," Cecily jumped in.

Megan couldn't let that one go. "A real man doesn't need to prove himself by imposing his wants and needs on—"

"We've got Sandy on line three," said Cecily. "Go ahead Sandy."

"Mr. O'Patrick?"

"Yes, Sandy?"

Sandy let out a breathy, little sigh. "I think you are just the sexiest man alive."

Megan nearly groaned out loud.

"I'm five foot two," Sandy continued, "blonde, a hundred and five—"

"Sandy," Megan interrupted.

"Call me. My number is 555—"

The producer was quick on the draw, and cut off the line before the greater Denver area could learn Sandy's home phone number.

"Friend of yours?" asked Megan. She should have guessed that Collin would stack the callers.

"Not yet."

Sandy was exactly the kind of woman guys like Collin went for. Naïve, insecure and needy. Ironically, she was also exactly the kind of woman who could benefit most from Megan and Cecily's book. "If you're still listening, Sandy," Megan spoke into the microphone, "send your mailing address to the station, and we'll provide you with a free copy of *The Perfect Boyfriend*."

"So you can indoctrinate one more man-hater?" asked Collin.

"So we can save an innocent woman from a life of simpering and servitude."

"We have Robin on one," said Cecily.

Robin, it turned out, was a man.

"Great goal on Sunday, Collin," he said.

"Thank you, Robin."

"And good on you for giving these man-haters the what-for. My wife read that rag, and she's been hell to live with ever since. Gripin' about the dishes. Gripin' about the kids. Gets so a guy can't even have a beer in peace anymore."

A brief expression of unease crossed Collin's face, but he quickly erased it. "Man deserves a little peace and quiet while he enjoys a beer," he said heartily.

Megan didn't know why it surprised her that Collin aligned himself with the redneck. She tried to keep her voice under control. "You're telling us that a woman should wash the dishes, take care of the kids and wait on a man hand and foot while he swills beer and watches sports all day Sunday?"

"I don't believe I used the word 'swill'."

"You're incredible," said Megan.

"Funny," Collin retorted, "I was thinking the same thing about you."

"I pity your girlfriend."

"I don't have a girlfriend."

Megan shot him a triumphant look. "Grab a clue, O'Patrick. There's a reason for that."

"I don't have a girlfriend because I travel too much."

"That your story?"

"I've *had* offers."

"Is that what you call them?"

"It might amaze you to discover this, but not all

women are demented dominatrixes who demand a man lick their boots—"

"Demented?"

Collin grinned and shook his head.

Yeah, yeah. She got it. She hadn't reacted to the word dominatrix. An image of the black bra flashed in her mind.

"Looks like Amy is our next caller," said Cecily. "Go ahead, Amy."

"Am I on the air?"

"Yes, you are."

"Oh, good. I wanted to ask Collin exactly what qualities he thinks attract women, since he's so sure it's not being a good listener, bringing flowers and laughing at their jokes?"

At last, one of their true listeners. A smile grew on Megan's face as she tipped her head sideways, waiting for Collin's response.

"Women want a man who is strong, independent and sticks to his values," said Collin.

"What if his values are different than hers?" asked Megan.

"Then, I guess, they argue."

"No compromise?"

"By compromise, do you mean swaying like a willow to her whims?"

"By independent, do you mean stopping for a beer with the guys instead of coming home?"

"Yeah. Sure. If he feels like it."

"What if she's cooked dinner?"

"What? He should call every night to make sure she hasn't planned his life for him?"

"There's such a thing as common courtesy."

"There's such a thing as being…whipped."

"Next caller," sang Cecily.

"I'd like to follow up on Amy's question," said the caller.

"Go ahead," invited Cecily.

Megan took a breath, glad the tide had turned. A sympathetic caller would give her a chance to regroup. Collin was even worse than she'd thought. Not only did he spout narcissistic nonsense, he seemed to genuinely believe it.

"Collin's saying that strength and independence will attract a woman," said the caller. "Megan believes kindness, respect and adoration are the only way to her heart."

"Correct," said Megan. Kindness, respect and adoration went a long way in this world.

"I think we should test the theories," said the caller.

"Test them how?" asked Cecily, glancing back and forth between Megan and Collin.

"Pit them against each other."

Cecily wiggled forward in her chair, looking entirely too eager at the prospect. "How do we do that?"

"Send Collin and Megan on a date."

"Together?" Megan squeaked, feeling her eyes go wide.

"Let's see if Megan is susceptible to his charms when he *doesn't* use anything on the list."

An entire evening with Collin? They'd be lucky if one of them was left standing.

Collin frantically shook his head, making a slashing motion across his throat.

"Yes!" came the producer's voice in Megan's ear.

Cecily's eyes twinkled. "It has definite possibilities."

"If Collin gets to first base," explained the caller, "he wins. If Megan resists his charm, she wins."

"But—"

"We'll do it," said Cecily as the strains of Aretha's "Respect" came up to end the show.

Outside the studio, Collin swung open the passenger door of Brett's sports car and climbed into the low-slung seat.

"Good thing you didn't get roped into a publicity stunt or anything." Brett smirked as he stuffed the transmission into first and pulled into the lights and traffic of Colfax Street.

"After we went off the air, I told them I wouldn't do it," said Collin. There was a certain satisfaction in getting his point across in a public way, but he had no desire to belabor the situation. The radio show was exactly the kind of exposure he hated.

Brett nodded, flipping on his left-turn signal to change lanes. "Diabolically brilliant."

"Brilliant?"

"Make them beg for it before you give in."

Collin pulled back and stared at Brett's profile. "Make who beg for what?"

"The audience, of course. Between your fans and Megan's listeners, half of Denver heard that dare. They'll be calling the station steady until you give in.

Whip 'em up into a frenzy, I say. Milk the publicity for all it's worth."

Collin's stomach clenched. "That's not—"

"Couldn't have orchestrated it better myself."

Damn it. Brett's words rang true. This had the potential to turn into a media circus.

"Give me your cell phone," said Collin.

Brett reached into his breast pocket. "Why?"

Collin snatched the phone. "Let's get this over with."

"You've changed your mind?" Brett asked with mock innocence.

Collin fished in his pocket for the number of the station. "Of *course* I've changed my mind. I'm not whipping anybody into a frenzy."

"Coach would love it."

"Coach can stuff it."

Brett gave an exaggerated sigh as he zipped across traffic, making a left through a busy intersection. "It pains me to see you squander your opportunities."

Collin carefully pressed the tiny numbers on the slim phone. "My name is not for sale."

"Nobody wants to buy your name… They just want to rent it."

"I'm not having any part of that racket." He and Brett had been through this argument before. Collin hated the thought of kids growing up miserable because their family couldn't afford the latest, overpriced *Collin O'Patrick* wear.

"Saint Collin of Denver," said Brett.

"Of Killarney," Collin exaggerated his Irish accent.

"And I'm getting it done as quickly and quietly as possible."

"You want to borrow my Harley?"

"Now that'll be quiet."

"I have never, repeat, *never* missed getting to first base when I took a woman out on my Harley."

Collin shook his head and gave a dry chuckle. Getting to first base was the last thing on his mind. He just wanted to end the damn thing.

"Never missed second base, either, for that matter," Brett mused.

"I just want to get the date over with and let the publicity die down."

"You have to win," said Brett.

"Right. With all due respect to your motorcycle, there's no way in the world Megan's going to kiss me."

"With all due respect to your much-touted principles, haven't you learned *anything* from me? Take the Harley. Kiss the woman. Vindicate athletes everywhere."

The station switchboard rang busy, so Collin punched the end button on the phone. "She doesn't seem like the type to be bowled over by black leather."

Brett gave him a look that questioned his intelligence. "Notwithstanding the fact that *all* women are bowled over by black leather, she'll be straddling a vibrating motorcycle…"

Collin grimaced. "You have no class."

"Hard to believe so many women go for me, isn't it?"

"I'm not using your Harley to turn Megan on so she'll kiss me."

Brett pulled a piece of paper out of the console. "Okay. Let's try this. I thought you had to do the opposite of the list?"

"I do."

"This list says women like classy, imported vehicles. Your Lexus is on her list. My Harley, on the other hand, is neither classy nor imported."

Collin stabbed redial. "How the hell did I get myself into this mess?"

"You're Saint Collin, defending the honor of the professional athlete."

"Next time I start strapping on the shining armor, kick me, will you?"

"You kidding? This is the best thing you've done for your career in years."

Collin grunted. This had nothing to do with his career. His career was on the soccer field, not in the media.

"You sure you're going to be able to handle this guy?" asked Cecily, talking around a mouthful of pins as she worked her way along the hem of Megan's slacks. They'd done this a hundred times before, Megan standing on her scarred end table, modeling one of Cecily's fashion creations, while Cecily worked on the finishing touches.

Megan spoke to the top of Cecily's head. "Of course I'll be able to handle him. He's a conceited jock."

"But he's a really sexy conceited jock."

"Well, since I'm not attracted to conceited jocks, sexy or otherwise, I think we're safe."

"You're not going to kiss him?"

"Puh-lease."

"Turn."

Megan shuffled in a circle. "You think I'm one of his groupies?"

"I think you haven't been with a man in months."

"That's because I've raised my standards. So have you."

"I'm just glad it's not me dating Collin O'Patrick for all the marbles. We're going to lose credibility big time if you kiss him."

"I'm not going to kiss him."

Cecily sat back on her heels. "Done."

"Great." Megan climbed down from the table onto the smooth hardwood floor of her apartment, glancing at her watch. "He's supposed to pick me up at six, but I think we can assume he'll be at least an hour late."

The Perfect Boyfriend list specifically required punctuality.

Cecily got to her feet, gathering her sewing supplies and putting them away in the kit that was open on Megan's coffee table. "What are you wearing?"

Megan slipped out of the suit pants, handing them to Cecily. "I can't decide whether to go with grunge or goth."

Cecily grinned. "Defensive clothing? Thought you said you weren't attracted to him?"

"No harm in making *me* unattractive to *him*, too. You know, just as a little insurance policy."

"Grunge," said Cecily. "Definitely grunge."

"Right." Megan nodded sharply. "I'll check the laundry hamper."

"I'm going to run this stuff across the hall, then I'll help you mess up your hair."

Megan headed into her compact bathroom, giving Cecily a wave goodbye. The two apartments had once been an opulent hotel suite, and shared a common foyer that was separate from the main hall of the former hotel.

Developers had cut the original suite in half, giving Megan a huge living room and Cecily a massive bedroom. Both apartments had tiny kitchens and minuscule bathrooms. But the high ceilings were gorgeous, and the location—near Sixteenth Street Mall—was close to shops, clubs and the shuttle.

In her tank top and panties, Megan rooted through her plastic laundry hamper, finding a pair of jeans with torn knees and a day-old, mustard-yellow wraparound top. It smelled a little stale, but she could stand it for an evening.

Socks were unnecessary. She'd slip into her clunky old sandals. Too bad she and Cecily had given each other pedicures yesterday. Cracked nail polish would have worked better. But she wasn't willing to sacrifice her gleaming magenta.

She straightened and glanced at her hair in the mirror. When she spent time with the blow-dryer, her blonde curls came out soft and pretty. But when she let her hair dry naturally, as she had today, it looked as if it had barely survived a hurricane.

Perfect.

Clothing scrunched in a ball in her arms, she headed

back out of the bathroom. "Sure hope he's taking me somewhere expensive," she called to Cecily.

"Afraid he's not," came a masculine voice.

Megan's bare feet skidded to a halt on the polished wood floor. Her eyes widened as she focused on Collin. Unshaven once again, he was wearing black cargo pants, a green T-shirt and a worn leather jacket draped over his broad shoulders. Good thing she wasn't attracted to bad boys.

"The door was open," he said, gesturing to her living-room door that led to the shared foyer.

Cecily appeared in the doorway behind him. "Oops. Sorry. I was only going to be a second."

"You're early," Megan accused Collin, ignoring the way his gaze followed the curve of her bare legs. Thank goodness she'd also shaved them when they did their pedicures. "You're supposed to be at least fifteen minutes late."

He shrugged. "The list says women like a man who's on time. I'm *not* on time."

"That's cheating."

"Cheating how? You saying you want men to be early?"

"No."

"Then I'm holding up my end of the bargain. I'm *not* acting like the perfect boyfriend."

Megan sighed. Fine. The jerkier he acted, the better for her. "Turn around," she commanded.

A lazy smile grew on his face and his gaze took in her legs once more. "Too late to save your modesty."

"They're legs, Collin."

"That they are, sweetheart."

"I'm about to turn around and walk into my room. It's a little early in the relationship for you to see my butt."

"You wearing a thong?"

"No."

"Then I'm not going to see anything."

"Turn around."

"Would the perfect boyfriend turn around?"

"Yes."

Collin's grin widened.

"Go to hell." Megan stomped toward her bedroom, refusing to try to cover up with the bundle of clothing. The pale blue briefs were hardly Victoria's Secret.

CHAPTER THREE

"NICE ass," Collin called, enjoying the emotion in the sharp slam of Megan's bedroom door. Let her be angry. As far as he was concerned, it was her fault that he was in this mess.

Out of the corner of his eye he could see Cecily valiantly holding back laughter.

He crossed his arms and cocked his head toward Megan's closed door. "How would you say I'm doin' so far?"

"Depends on whether you want her to kiss you or kill you."

"I think we both know she's not going to kiss me." He cracked a half-smile. "I'm just trying to drive her crazy."

"Then you're batting a thousand."

"I'm a soccer player."

"Scoring a thousand?"

"Close enough."

Cecily clicked Megan's apartment door shut behind her and crossed to a small couch in the far corner of the combination dining and living room. A burgundy-hued area rug covered the living-room section, and the walls were papered with bright travel posters. Ferns and palm trees crept in from the corners.

"So, where are you taking her?" asked Cecily, settling back, her feet curled beneath her.

Collin shook his head. "Surprise."

"She hates sushi."

"So do I."

The bedroom door creaked behind him.

"There you go," said Cecily. "Something in common already."

"I like sex," said Collin.

"Excuse me?" came Megan's voice.

Cecily's voice brightened. "So does Megan."

"*Excuse* me?"

Collin turned around in time to see Megan's eyebrows nearly hit her hairline.

"Ask her about her leather underwear," said Cecily.

"Definitely." Collin meant it. She might be sporting a bag-lady look, but he'd seen enough skin earlier to know he'd willingly take a look at any kind of underwear she cared to put on.

"Whose side are you on?" Megan asked Cecily, picking her keys up from a table next to the wall. Then she turned her attention to Collin. "Should I bring my credit card?"

"Does the list say I have to pay?" asked Collin.

"Definitely."

"Better bring it along."

She made a disgusted sound in the back of her throat.

He crossed the room to open the door. "Just trying to stick to the rules."

Megan grabbed a multicolored sweater from one of the dining-room chairs and sailed past him. "Uncouth seems to come naturally to you."

"You two kids have fun," Cecily called.

Collin turned around and winked at her. He was beginning to like Cecily.

They exited through the foyer into the hall, then down the flight of stairs to the sidewalk.

"Which way to your car?" she asked, shrugging into the sweater. The bright colors made her outfit look even more bizarre.

She pulled her rat's nest of hair from the collar as Collin pointed to Brett's Harley.

"That's a motorcycle."

"It's domestic," said Collin, picking up the extra helmet and holding it out for her.

Megan slid him a glance he was becoming familiar with.

"Your list said women liked classy and imported."

Her expression didn't change.

"I went with rough and domestic."

She closed her eyes for a second, shaking her head in a gesture of denial.

He held out a helmet.

She gazed at it in disgust. "I don't think so."

"Can't hurt," he said.

Her eyes narrowed quizzically.

He nodded to her hair. "How long did it take you to get it that way?"

"It's the latest."

Collin grinned. "If bed-head is the latest, helmet-hair's got to be up and coming."

"Are you always such a smooth talker?"

"Are you always such a classy dresser?"

She blinked her long, dark lashes. "I thought this outfit up special. Just for you."

"That was very sweet. But unless you want to show up on the news in it, I'd get on the bike."

"The news?"

"I don't know about you, but I'm thinking the press knows our date's been set for six, and I'm getting a little worried about company."

Megan glanced around uneasily. Then she grabbed the helmet and stuffed it over her hair. "Right." She straddled the bike seat.

"Now we're talking," said Collin, climbing on in front of her.

He kicked the giant vibrator into action.

Collin cruised along Colfax Street toward Lookout Mountain Road. Brett's Harley was a darn sight bigger than the European bikes he'd grown up on in Killarney. But the principle was the same. And he had to admit the feel of rumbling power between his legs gave him a rush.

When he leaned into the first corner, Megan's arms clamped around his waist. That gave him a rush, too.

She might be tart and unreasonable, but she was also

soft and curvy and warm against his back. It had been a while since a woman had clung to him, longer still since he'd been to bed with anybody. And even though he knew this date was going exactly nowhere, he couldn't help the images of Megan and tangled bed sheets that formed in his mind.

He didn't fight them. Their ride up into the mountains would end soon enough, and Megan would open her mouth and shatter the fantasy. So for now he settled into the winding curves, poured on the power, and let his mind wander over pleasant, scintillating territory.

Forty-five minutes out of the city, Megan started to wonder where the hell Collin was taking her. They'd turned off Lookout Mountain Road a few miles back, climbing higher into the Rockies. It was too early for skiing or snowboarding, and he hadn't asked her if she knew how to hang glide. Maybe his idea of a hot date was mountain-goat viewing?

She adjusted her butt on the leather seat. Whatever, just as long as they got there, got it done, and ended this date with her the winner. She was going on air next week with one more victory for womankind. And showing Collin up wouldn't hurt the show's reputation either.

The drive dragged on, while the road narrowed and the mountain peaks and cedar trees closed in on both sides. Megan shifted again.

She'd admit that riding a Harley had been a bit of a thrill at first. She'd even go so far as to say it was sexy. But once her butt had fallen asleep, the romance had faded and she'd started wishing Collin would get to the date, already.

Then they rounded a long curve, and the forest parted. The darkening sky widened, revealing a small town clustered along the roadway between snowy mountain peaks.

Collin geared down and leaned the bike to the left, turning into the parking lot of an aging gas station. They bumped through a loose patch of gravel where the concrete driveway had long since crumbled away. He stopped the Harley next to a stained white pump beneath a wide awning and kicked out the bike stand.

Megan didn't wait for an invitation to climb off. Her inner thighs tingled in protest as she straightened and brought them together for the first time in over an hour.

Collin swung his leg over the seat and strode to the pump. The cool alpine wind gusted across the quiet street, blowing stray hair into her eyes and swaying the round gas-station sign suspended high above the lot entrance. Its rusty chain creaked in the quiet.

Nobody came out of the building to help them, though a dog barked lackadaisically from behind the wooden fence of the yard next door.

"Charming little out-of-the-way nouvelle cuisine?" she inquired, shading her eyes against the setting sun to gaze around the minitown.

Collin lifted the red-handled nozzle, worn dark from thousands of hands before his. He flipped a metal lever, and the pump groaned to life. "Nope. Gas."

Megan shifted her attention back to Collin. "You mean we're not there yet?"

"Afraid not."

"We stopped for *gas*."

"We did."

Yellow plastic balls spun madly inside a glass bubble stuck on the side of the pump, while mechanical numbers clicked over in rapid succession.

"How far are we going?" she asked, beginning to get annoyed.

"Let's just say it's a surprise," he drawled.

Megan crossed her arms over her chunky sweater. The snowy peaks were still a thousand feet above them, but the air was cooling off with the altitude. "I don't like surprises."

"Wasn't there something about 'little surprises' on The Perfect Boyfriend list?"

"We were referring to jewelry. Expensive jewelry."

Collin stopped the pump on four-nine-five. "Dreamer."

She shrugged. "Some guys like buying their girl-friends jewelry."

"Well, in the interest of disobeying the rules, tonight I'm going for a big surprise instead of a little one."

Megan stared at the price on the pump. If five bucks had brought them this far, he must be planning to take her all the way to Chicago on a full tank.

"Maybe this wasn't such a good idea," she ventured. After all, what did she really know about the guy?

His eyebrows went up. "What wasn't such a good idea?"

"This date." He could be planning anything, be taking her anywhere.

"It was *your* idea," Collin pointed out.

"It was that caller's idea." Maybe he was an ax-murdering soccer player planning to dump her body across the state line.

"Well, the caller came up with the idea on *your* show," he said.

"As I recall, I said no to the idea." Did they murder people in Nebraska?

"So did I," he said.

"Yet, here we are."

"Here we are," Collin agreed.

Megan assessed him for a moment. Since half the population of Denver knew they were together, he could hardly come back alone with no explanation.

She supposed she was safe enough.

Didn't mean she had to like it.

"Our deal was for a date, not a road trip."

"Fifteen more minutes, and we're there."

Tires crunched on the gravel shoulder behind her, and Collin's gaze flicked past her left ear to take in the vehicle. "Maybe ten," he said.

Before Megan had a chance to make him swear to that, the screen door to the gas station banged open. A fiftyish, balding man in a pair of faded gray coveralls emerged.

"Can I help you folks?" he called as he made his way toward them.

"Owe you five bucks," Collin called back, pulling a bill from his pocket and taking a couple of steps to meet the man.

"Check your oil?" the man asked.

"We've got it covered." Collin nodded.

"Y'all have a good trip, then."

"Thanks." Collin stepped backward and gave the man a wave. Then he paused beside Megan, shoulder nearly brushing hers as he muttered under his breath, "You think you can hang on tight?"

"I've *been* hanging on tight since we left," she answered, noting the time on her watch. Collin had fifteen minutes' grace, and not a second more.

He tipped his head slightly toward her, gray eyes catching her gaze. "I mean *really* tight."

Megan stilled, staring into the flinty depths. "Why?" How far was he planning to take her in fifteen minutes?

"Don't look when I say this—"

"Look at what?"

"Keep looking at me."

"Are you…sane?"

"There's a reporter following us."

Megan reflexively glanced to where the tires had sounded on the road's shoulder.

Collin's hand quickly rose to her cheek, gently but firmly stopping her head from turning. "I *told* you not to look."

"Sorry." She shifted away from the warmth of his palm.

"I'm going to lose him," said Collin.

Megan felt her eyes go wide. "Like a car chase?"

He nodded. "Like a car chase. Only he hasn't got a chance, because we're on a bike."

She shook her head. "Uh uh."

"I'm a good rider."

"No way."

"Piece of cake."

"Take me home."

"If I take you home, *Carl Bernstein* over there is going to report that we didn't have a date. And then your listeners are going to call in, and my fans will get in on the act. And pretty soon the whole damn state of Colorado will whip itself into a frenzy, and I'll be pushing sneakers and T-shirts on NBC."

"Huh?"

"Get on the bike."

"You're not turning me into a smudge on the asphalt."

"I'm a professional athlete with the reflexes of a jungle cat."

"No dice."

"If you won't trust my reflexes, trust my sense of self-preservation."

"Oh, yeah. Like that's going to sway me."

"I lay this bike over, first thing that breaks is my leg."

"Don't you mean *my* leg?"

"A broken leg destroys my season, probably my career."

"And here *I* was only worried about the pain and the mess."

Collin fought a grin. "There won't be any pain and mess, I promise. I'm good. Get on the bike."

Megan sighed in frustration. "Whatever happened to dinner and a movie?"

"Dinner and a movie were on The Perfect Boyfriend list. Though I did consider corn dogs and *Freddie versus Godzilla*."

Megan gritted her teeth, steeling herself against his mocking charm.

His cock-eyed grin *wasn't* cute. And his juvenile joke wasn't funny. And his gray eyes *weren't* twinkling in the sunset. And she *was* a fool to trust him.

"You could always kiss me now," said Collin. "Let Bernstein get a picture. And then we can all go home."

"Let you win?"

Collin gave a lazy shrug. "Sure. Why not?"

"It would kill my ratings." She glanced from Collin to the bike, then surreptitiously to the road.

She gritted her teeth even harder. Hell, she'd been a fool for most of her life. Why stop now? She swung her leg over the seat and settled her tired butt on the stiff leather.

Collin slipped in front of her, twisting his head over his shoulder. "So, out of all my logical arguments, you risk your life for ratings?"

"You kill me, and you'll be sorry."

She heard his warm chuckle for a split second before the bike roared to life. She quickly wrapped her arms around his waist, snuggling her crotch up against his butt and plastering her chest to his back. Her thighs bracketed his body in a distinctly sexual way. But there were times in a woman's life when modesty went out the window, and this was definitely one of them.

He poured on the power, and she tightened her grip as the engine roared to a crescendo. They rocketed from under the awning.

Out on the road, the big motor whapped and crackled as Collin worked his way through the gears. Their speed moved well past eighty, and the mountain scenery flashed by.

Surprisingly, Megan's fear was replaced by exhilaration. Though she wasn't completely convinced they'd make it out alive, the bike felt solid on the road, and Collin's movements seemed focused and confident. They quickly left the little township and everything else in their dust.

His muscles shifted against her, and body heat built between them from the friction of his leather jacket. She might not have a secret bad-boy fantasy going, but apparently she had a secret daredevil fantasy. The wind buffeted her clothes, sensitizing her skin as her mind catalogued every facet of Collin's body.

This time, the ride was too short.

They came to a bigger town, and Collin slowed the bike. He zipped around a few corners until they were well out of sight of the highway. With luck, the reporter would keep going straight on through.

They rolled past a Tastee Freeze, skirted a supermarket, headed through two traffic lights, then pulled into a dirt parking lot next to a sprawling park. Collin maneuvered the motorcycle between a fence and a maintenance shack, where it was out of sight of the road. He killed the engine and pulled off his helmet.

"*This* is our date?" Megan shook off her humming arousal as she removed her own helmet. She fluffed her flat hair and finger-combed it back from her face. Then she glanced around at a dusky playground, a baseball field and a swimming pool.

Collin took the helmet from her hands. "This is our date."

She eased off the bike once more, not quite as stiff as she'd been the first time. "A picnic?"

"A soccer game."

"You're playing?"

He shook his head and gestured to the park gate. "It's a girl's game."

"Well, *I'm* not playing."

"Eighteen and under," said Collin.

Megan cleared her throat. "Oh." She started walking. "It's been a while since I was eighteen."

He fell into step beside her. "I guessed that."

She narrowed her eyes. "Your daughter playing?" she asked with syrupy sweetness.

"Yeah, right. She was conceived when I was ten."

"You're younger than you look," Megan countered without skipping a beat.

He paused to let her pass first through the gate. "I should have kissed you for the reporter and ended this."

"I'd have ducked."

"You forget, I have the reflexes of a jungle cat."

"You don't know it, but *I* have the reflexes of a UCLA co-ed."

Collin grinned, indicating a path that cut diagonally

across the park lawn. The lights of the soccer field were visible in the distance. "Have to give you that one."

"Thank you."

They were both silent for a moment.

"UCLA?" he asked.

"Marketing," she answered. "You?"

"Stanford. Philosophy."

"You're kidding."

"And soccer, of course."

"You have a philosophy degree?"

"Was that a note of respect?"

"You don't strike me as the intellectual type."

Collin paused, turning to face her, blocking her way on the mulch path. "Now that you know there's more to me than good looks, are you ready to kiss me?" He glanced from side to side. "We've lost the reporter."

She made to go around him, shaking her head. "I'm not going to kiss you." Not tonight, not ever. She was winning this challenge, for herself and for women everywhere. *Here me roar.*

He started walking backwards on the path. "Why not? I'm smart. I'm fit. I have a Harley and I know how to use it."

Megan fought a grin. "Oh, well, since you have a Harley, I'll throw my ratings out the window and give into your vibrating charm."

"Brett told me you'd say that."

"Brett?"

"A friend. The guy who owns the Harley."

"It's not yours?"

"Nope."

Megan pursed her lips in an exaggerated pout. "Then I guess I'll have to kiss Brett."

Collin snapped his fingers. "So close."

"So close," she agreed as they passed between two sets of bleachers.

The shouts from a sparse crowd of spectators grew louder, and the referee's whistle blasted through the air as the game fanned out before them. It was nearly dark, and the finely trimmed field glistened under the big lights as players fought for the checked ball, their ponytails bouncing with their jogging strides.

Collin led Megan to an empty spot on the benches.

"Who are we voting for?" she asked.

"It's not an election."

She slanted him a glare. "You know what I mean."

He nodded toward the game. "I sometimes help out with the Panthers. The purple team."

"You help out?"

"Don't sound so surprised. I'm a nice guy, as well as being an athlete and an intellectual."

Megan stared at him. "You serious, or is this a ploy to get me to like you?"

With a roll of his eyes, Collin stood up and cupped a hand beside his mouth. "Hey, Anna."

A woman, obviously the coach, turned at the sound of his voice. When she saw him, she smiled and waved.

Megan recognized the woman's face, and her heart did a little flip inside her chest.

"See," he said on a note of triumph, sitting back down.

"Anna Simpson?" asked Megan, barely believing it.

"You know her?"

"Anna Simpson, the starting center for the Olympic women's soccer team?"

Collin blinked in the bright lights. "You're a soccer fan?"

"Can you introduce me?"

Anna Simpson was on Megan's top-fifty list of people she'd like to sign for endorsements. She stayed away from bona fide celebrities, and tried to stick with up and comers—people who might realistically consider Point To Point ad agency.

Soccer was gaining popularity, and women's sports in general were garnering media attention. Megan could think of a dozen companies who might be willing to talk about an ad campaign that featured Anna Simpson. And if the team won a medal, the sky was the limit.

"Sure," said Collin as the small crowd roared its approval for a spectacular save. "I take it you don't have such a low opinion of female athletes?"

Megan tipped her chin down and peered at him from the tops of her eyes. "I don't have such a low opinion of females, period."

"You're a hard woman," said Collin as he stood up, moving into the aisle.

"We're going to meet her now?" Megan smoothed back her hair, wishing with all her heart she hadn't decided on the grunge look—Collin or no Collin.

He shook his head. "She's busy coaching."

"Then where are you going?" Having ditched the

reporter, and knowing she wouldn't kiss him, was he going to abandon her here?

"Refreshment stand," he answered

She tamped down her suspicions. "Oh. All right." It was nearly eight o'clock. Even a concession hot dog and a lukewarm cola sounded good to her about now.

Collin turned away.

After letting her gaze rest on his rear for the briefest of self-indulgent moments, she forced herself to look away. He was an athlete. Of course he was in good shape. And admiring his tight butt was a perfectly natural, hormonal reaction. It didn't mean she had the slightest interest in his brain.

A good butt did not make a good man.

She cleared the image from her mind and turned her attention to the young women on the field, watching as they dribbled the ball, passed, sprinted and shot at the wide net. They were alert, shouting instructions to one another, taking advantage of every opening.

They played hard.

They played smart.

And they played with confidence.

The world needed more teenagers like these. Megan couldn't imagine any of them putting up with crap from their boyfriends.

She heard Collin's boots on the wooden risers, and caught his shadow in her peripheral vision. She straightened, mouth watering at the thought of a broiled hot dog and a steamed bun.

He settled on the bench next to her, placing a single

drink cup on the opposite side. The cardboard box on his lap had one wrapped hot dog and a mound of fries.

Megan drew back, brows slanting together as she stared at him.

He popped a fry into his mouth, took a drink from the colorful paper cup and smiled as he unwrapped the hot dog.

Then he took a big bite.

"Good," he mumbled.

She stared at him, slack-jawed, not quite sure what to say.

He swallowed. "Something wrong?" He took another draw through the plastic straw.

The crowd cheered a turnover from the red team to the purple.

"I thought…"

"Thought what?" he asked.

She held up her palms in confusion. "Did you think I wasn't hungry?"

Collin cocked his head sideways, a dimple forming in one cheek. "Would the *perfect boyfriend* buy you refreshments?"

"Of *course*."

He treated her to an annoyingly self-satisfied grin, and stuffed another fry into his mouth, turning back to the game.

Megan swore colorfully under her breath.

"The perfect girlfriend wouldn't use words like that," he pointed out mildly.

"The perfect girlfriend would have stolen the motorcycle, dumped you at the gas station and saved the world from another aggravating male," Megan returned as she got up to buy her own food.

CHAPTER FOUR

THE Panthers lost three to two. But as Collin led Megan toward the bench to introduce her to Anna Simpson the players seemed in good spirits. He considered it a testament to Anna's coaching skills that her girls handled the loss with such composure.

"Hey, O'Patrick," called Dana Miller, dropping a soccer ball to her feet, juggling it once on each foot, twice on each knee, then heading it in his direction.

He caught it with his left foot. He was hampered by his clunky boots, but he managed to repeat her pattern, add an extra header and catch it on the back of his neck between his shoulder blades.

He flipped it back to her.

She matched his pattern, then one of the other girls called for the ball.

"I take it you know them," Megan observed beside him.

"Like I told you, I help Anna out sometimes."

"Collin," Anna greeted him, winding her way through the sea of teenage girls.

He held out his arms and pulled her into a hug. She wasn't a tall woman, but she was lithe, coordinated and fast as the wind.

She pulled back. "What did you think?"

"I think your defense fell apart when their striker got too close, but Natalie was on her game in left field. Where's Marilyn?"

"Hurt her ankle," said Anna.

Collin was sorry to hear that. "Bad?"

"Soft tissue. She'll be out for a couple of weeks at least."

Megan cleared her throat behind him.

He stepped to one side. "Anna Simpson. I'd like you to meet Megan Brock."

Megan moved forward with her hand outstretched. "It's a thrill to meet you, Anna."

Anna's mouth twitched up in a grin. "Megan Brock? As in Perfect Boyfriend Megan Brock?" Her gaze darted from Megan to Collin and back again.

"Guilty as charged," said Megan with a laugh.

"So this is it?" asked Anna. "*This* is the big date."

"This is the big date," said Megan.

Anna socked Collin in the shoulder. "You brought her to a soccer game?"

"Believe me," Megan interjected, "if I'd known I was going to meet you, I wouldn't have complained about the motorcycle ride."

Anna's voice rose half an octave. "You brought her all the way up here on a *motorcycle*?"

"Brett's Harley."

Her voice went even higher. "You took dating advice from *Brett*?"

"It was all worth it," Megan insisted.

"You're supposed to get her to kiss you," Anna nearly shrieked.

The players' conversation dipped, and there was a split second of silence.

"Hey, guys," one of them called, moving in closer. "O'Patrick's on his Perfect Boyfriend date."

"His date?" somebody repeated.

"*This* is his date?" asked another voice.

The girls clustered around.

"Are you Megan Brock?"

"Don't fall for his dimple."

"Did you kiss him yet?"

"No," Megan answered the final question in a clear voice.

Collin couldn't decide whether to laugh or shrink into the turf.

"You *gonna* kiss him?" Natalie asked from the rear of the pack, stretching up to see over her teammates.

"Not a chance," Megan called back good-naturedly.

"Right on, sister," came a voice that sounded suspiciously like Dana.

"You show 'im," said someone else.

"Hey," Collin protested. "After all I've done for you guys?"

"You're our hero," shouted Dana, obviously willing to play both sides.

"Thank you." Collin couldn't help but be grateful that somebody was backing him.

"I meant Megan," Dana corrected.

"Dana!"

"I mean, really, Collin," said Anna. "What woman wouldn't want a man who makes blender drinks?"

"But—" Collin protested.

"I'd run," Megan suggested to him in an undertone. "Now. Quick."

"These are my friends," Collin pointed out.

"They're also women."

He glanced around, suddenly feeling surrounded.

While he considered his options, Megan shifted closer to Anna, handing her a business card. "Ever give any thought to product endorsements?"

Anna's eyes went wide as she looked down at the square of cardboard.

"Like commercials?" asked Dana.

"Commercials would be cool," said Natalie, working her way closer.

Collin cringed at Anna's deer-in-the-headlights expression. "I'm *so* sorry, Anna—" he began.

"I have a small ad agency," said Megan, apparently oblivious to Collin's embarrassment and Anna's stupefaction. "The radio show is just a sideline—"

"Megan." Collin snapped in warning under his breath.

"I'm sure I could—"

"Back off," said Collin.

"—get you some celebrity endorsements—"

He wrapped his arm around Megan's waist, stopping her short.

"Can you imagine Coach on television?" said a player, her voice full of awe.

Megan grabbed at Collin's arm. "Let go of me."

He tugged her backward, giving the stunned Anna a quick wave of goodbye. "You're soliciting my friends," he rumbled in Megan's ear.

She kept struggling. "I'm offering her a business opportunity. Besides, they're on my side."

Collin kept backing up. "I didn't introduce you so you could come on like a snake-oil salesman."

"Hey, she could make a lot of money."

"Hey, she's not interested."

"How do you know that? You didn't even give her a chance to answer."

"I saw the expression on her face." Collin felt like a heel. As soon as he got home, he'd call Anna and apologize.

He turned, keeping a firm arm around Megan's waist, leading her back between the bleachers onto the park pathway.

"You're just mad because they're on my side," she grumbled.

"They're not on your side. They're teasing me." At least Collin hoped they were. He had to believe the bizarre boyfriend list only appealed to Megan's weirdo readers, not to a broad demographic.

"You can let go of me now," she said.

"Not a chance."

"What? You think I could out-sprint you?"

She had a point.

He loosened his grip. "We're going home."

"Fine with me."

"Don't you dare call her."

"Exactly who died and left you king?"

"Megan."

"I'm not selling time-share condos. She has my card. She can call me if she's interested."

Collin gave a sharp nod.

Unexpectedly, Megan grinned. "You didn't have to make such a big deal about it. I'm not carrying a bottle of Dr. McGillicuddy's elixir and a contract in my back pocket. All she had to do was say no."

"Dr. McGillicuddy's elixir?"

"You called me a snake-oil salesman."

Okay, so he might have overreacted just a little bit.

They were both silent as they made their way across the sparsely lit grass toward the bright parking lot. Clouds were rolling in, blocking the moon and the stars. The smell of impending rain hung in the air.

"You took me by surprise, that's all," he finally muttered.

"Most people are thrilled to have an ad agency offer them a possible job."

"Not all athletes want to be celebrities."

"Lots do."

They passed through the park gate and came to the motorcycle.

Collin picked up Megan's helmet. "That's their problem."

She took it from his hands. "Problem?"

"I happen to think selling your name is tacky."

Megan chuckled as she pulled the helmet onto her head. "I happen to think selling your name is profitable. Especially when you can sell it over and over and over again. Think about it, Collin." She rubbed her thumb and fingertips together. "It's like selling air. It's not really there in the first place, and it's unlimited."

Collin climbed onto the bike as thunder rumbled far away in the mountain peaks. "It doesn't get any more real than your good name and your reputation."

"How does selling a sports drink or a pair of jogging shoes tarnish your reputation?"

Collin didn't want to have this argument, so instead of answering he started the motorcycle.

They were about three miles down the road when the first fat raindrops splatted on the back of Megan's neck. Lightning flashed against the distant peaks and rolling thunder competed with the engine as the Harley's headlight sliced through the darkness of the mountain road.

Megan hunched forward, hoping Collin's broad shoulders and the hard-shelled helmet would help protect her from the storm.

He geared down, pulling the bike off to the side of the deserted road. When it had rolled to a stop he put out the kickstand, leaving the engine running. The beam of the headlight angled off across the highway and into the dense bush.

"What are you doing?" she shouted over the noise, not sure if he would hear her under his helmet.

He hopped off and shrugged out of his leather jacket despite the increasing rain, holding it out to her. "Put it on," he yelled.

"What?" she asked, trying not to get distracted by his sculpted chest and biceps. Her fixation with his body was pathetic. She really needed to get out on more dates.

Another lightning strike bounced off the mountain-side, highlighting the wet, dappled pattern forming on his green T-shirt. He was going to be soaked in about two minutes.

Collin pushed the jacket into her hands. "Put it on."

She pushed back. "You need it. I've got a sweater."

He shot her a look of impatience. "Your sweater will soak right through."

"So will your shirt."

"I am *not* covering up while my date freezes her ass off."

"You mean there's actually a limit to the jerk-face things you're willing to do to me?"

His jaw tightened. "I knew we'd be on a bike. I should have warned you. Take the damn jacket."

Megan paused. He did have a point. This *was* all his fault. And the thought of staying dry was tempting.

Fine. She scooped the big jacket out of his hands, zipping it over her sweater before the argument about who should stay dry became a moot point. Turning up the collar, she adjusted the wide elastic band across her butt. The sleeves were long enough to cover her fingertips, and heat quickly built in the generous airspace around her body.

"Thank you," she mumbled.

Collin gave her a curt nod and remounted the bike. His strong, bare forearms glistened in the driving rain, muscles flexing as he pulled back onto the highway and brought the bike up to speed.

Crouched behind his back, protected from the worst of the wind and rain, and toasty warm inside the jacket, Megan wondered if she should add *give up your clothing* to The Perfect Boyfriend list. Of course a criterion like that could be interpreted any number of ways. None of which was bad…

The thunderclouds closed in on top of them. Sparse raindrops turned to a torrent, and Collin was forced to slow the bike. It was half an hour before the lights of the little gas station came into view.

He pulled under the canopy and killed the bike engine. They both removed their helmets.

"We need gas again?" asked Megan, scrunching her hair with her fingertips, attempting damage control on the bad-hair day to end all bad-hair days.

Collin shook his head. "I was hoping they'd have a coffee shop or something open."

"Doesn't look like it," she said, taking in the dark buildings. "You cold?"

He got off the bike. "I'm fine. But driving's a bitch in this. You?"

"I'm pretty warm."

"Your legs okay?"

"Wet, but I'll live."

He nodded. "Might as well wait here for a few minutes and see if the worst of it lets up."

Megan got off the bike. "Sounds good to me."

She checked out the front of the stained stucco building, hoping for a coffee vending machine. They weren't getting any wetter under the canopy, but the wind was up, and a hot drink would definitely help. She caught a trace of movement in the front of the door, and instinctively jumped toward Collin. "What's that?"

"What's what?"

"By the door. There." She pointed.

Collin leaned forward, squinting. He took a few steps toward the building.

"Be careful," said Megan. They were practically out in the wilderness here.

"Whatever it is, it's not very big," Collin pointed out.

But Megan wasn't convinced they could see all of it. Could be the paw of a giant bear lurking behind the freezer. Or maybe it had friends. She peered into the murky darkness, a shiver running up her spine.

Thunder rumbled again, and the thing made a noise. A whimper. Was it hurt?

Hadn't she read that wild animals lashed out when they were hurt? "Collin—"

"It's a puppy."

"A puppy?"

"A puppy."

"What's a puppy doing out here?"

Collin bent over and scooped the little creature into

his arms. "Must have accidentally been left outside." He rattled the door of the gas-station building. "Maybe he's a guard dog in training."

"What kind of dog?" If it was a baby wolf, its mother could be nearby. And its father, maybe even aunts and uncles. She'd watched *Wild Kingdom*. She knew these things ran in packs.

Collin rattled the locked door again, peering into the window. "I don't know. Black. Floppy ears. Square nose. What does it matter?"

Didn't sound like a wolf. Not that she was an expert. "I was just wondering. You know, if he was a guard dog."

"I'm going to check around the back."

"What for?"

"There's a house back there."

Before Megan could decide whether to go with him or stay out here by herself, he disappeared around the side of the building. With a furtive glance around her, Megan leaned against the motorcycle, pulling her hands up into the sleeves of the jacket.

She didn't like this. Not one bit. She was a city girl. She liked walls. And what she couldn't see made her nervous.

Flashes of lightning illuminated the deserted town, while thunder echoed eerily through the valley. Rain crashed down in waves on the canopy roof, muting the sounds of anything else that might be happening around her, anything else that might be sneaking up on her.

She shifted, and her wet blue jeans sucked against her thighs. Tiny rivulets of water trickled from her hair past the collar of Collin's jacket and slipped down her spine. This was definitely the worst date she'd ever been on.

As the minutes ticked by she got angry with Collin.

Still, she was grateful when he appeared from behind the building. As he grew closer she realized he still had the puppy in his arms. Pure black and covered in fuzzy, damp fur, it was lying across one forearm, ungainly paws sticking out in front, square nose wrinkling, dark eyes taking in everything around it. Its eyebrows quirked as it focused on Megan, then they slanted together for a moment as if she worried him.

After a couple of seconds, his face relaxed and he gazed at her with friendly adoration.

Megan didn't consider herself a sap, and dogs had certainly never been part of her life growing up in downtown Denver, but when the pathetic little guy yawned in her direction she decided he had to be the sweetest thing she'd ever seen.

"What happened?" she asked.

Collin came to a stop, scratching the pup behind one ear. "Owner found him a week ago. Figured he got left behind by a tourist. They've been feeding him, but they can't take him in the house because his wife's allergic."

Megan felt a rush of pity. "Aww."

"Said he had a basket out here to sleep in."

Megan glanced at the sheet of water falling on the parking lot and thought about the snow creeping down the mountains. She wouldn't want to be sleeping in a basket out here.

Collin nodded toward her chest. "Think you can fit him in there?"

Megan looked down. "Where?"

"Zip him inside my jacket. It'll keep your hands free and him warm while we're out on the highway."

Megan couldn't believe what she was hearing. "You're dog-napping him?"

"I'm liberating him."

"But, you can't…"

Collin moved forward, tugging on the metal zipper. "Hey, it's not like he's slobbery or anything."

The perfect boyfriend will love my mother, my senile grandmother and my slobbery dog.

"Did you memorize the list?" she asked.

"Wasn't I supposed to?"

A funny feeling tightened Megan's chest, and she didn't stop him as he slipped the puppy inside the jacket. The backs of his hands brushed against her ribcage.

"You're going to keep him?"

"Sure. Why not?" Collin caught her gaze, and she sucked in a deep breath at the tender expression in his eyes.

The puppy squirmed against her, settling itself in the minihammock that was the bottom of the jacket.

"I…" She was losing it here.

He smiled at the puppy's movements. "I *think* he'll go to sleep."

The tender smile tugged at Megan's heart. "He'll be fine."

"You don't mind?" His voice was low and husky.

Megan licked her lips. "No."

This time the tender smile was for her. "Thanks."

Megan's pulse sped up, awareness buzzing through her body. Collin's dark lips started looking very interesting.

She couldn't kiss Collin. The entire point of this evening was *not* kissing Collin.

Sure, he'd rescued a sweet little puppy. And sure, he'd given her his jacket. And sure, he helped with a teenage girls' soccer team and had tried to protect Anna when he'd thought Megan was taking advantage of her. But those things only made him four notches up from a bottom-of-the-basement jerk.

"You're my kinda date," he said.

"Rain-soaked?"

"No. A partner in crime."

The puppy flipped over one more time, then let out a shuddering sigh.

"You're going to have to feed him and walk him and train him for the next fifteen years," Megan warned, trying to keep her heart from melting over the warm, vulnerable bundle cuddled up next to her tummy and the strong, soaking-wet man standing in front of her.

"I think the little guy needs a break."

Oh, hell.

Megan's skin began to tingle and her breathing turned shallow. The man was temptation on wheels. Two, to be exact.

Collin pushed a strand of wet hair away from her cheek. His fingertips were rough and warm and entirely masculine. It had been a long time since a man had touched her with such tenderness.

Minty breath fanned her face. His lips parted and his gaze softened. He leaned almost imperceptibly closer.

Maybe she could kiss him and lie about it later. It would be his word against hers. Who would know?

"Megan," he breathed.

Lightning crackled far away, and the echoing thunder sent a primitive rumble through her body.

She touched his cold, bare arm, steadying herself as she stretched toward his lips. How would they feel? How would they taste? How long would he kiss her?

Lightning flashed in her eyes, so close and bright she recoiled.

"What the hell?" Collin practically shouted.

The puppy jerked reflexively inside the jacket, his big paws scrabbling against her shirt.

Megan's arms automatically went around him.

She heard footsteps hitting the concrete, and turned to see a man sprint across a wide ditch and jump into his car.

"The reporter," said Collin on a note of disgust.

Megan pulled herself back, her softer feelings for Collin instantly evaporating. "Surprise, surprise, surprise," she sneered. "Did you plant the puppy, too?"

Collin turned to look at her. "Huh?"

Megan gave a short, self-deprecating chuckle as she shook her head, reaching for the zipper. She had to hand it to him: he was diabolically brilliant. Of course, it might have been his agent and his teammates who thought up the plan. Maybe Anna was in on it too.

If Anna was in on it, Megan's chances of getting a new celebrity client were zero.

As she started to unzip the coat Collin's hand closed over hers.

"I didn't plan any of this," he insisted.

"Right." Megan might be a little slow on the uptake, but she tried to learn a little bit faster than your average invertebrate.

"I'm taking the puppy home," said Collin.

Megan glared at him with suspicion. "Why? Was it already yours?"

"No! Of course not. What kind of a man do you think I am?"

"A man who'd play on my sympathies to win a stupid radio contest."

"I didn't play on your sympathies."

"And the reporter just happened to be waiting here?"

"This is where he lost us on the way up. Makes sense that he'd stake it out."

Megan gave a snort of disbelief.

"You think I planned the storm, too?" asked Collin.

"I wouldn't put anything past you," she said, feeling more foolish by the second. At least she hadn't really kissed him. Though she'd been about to. And that picture was going to be damning evidence against her.

CHAPTER FIVE

MEGAN pushed Cecily's apartment door shut behind her and leaned back, resting her head on its solid strength. "I think we're going to have to get a group rate on hit men." She sighed.

Cecily quirked a smile. "Uh oh. What did he do?"

Megan straightened away from the door, raking her limp hair back from her face and wrinkled her nose at the combination of laundry-hamper shirt and wet dog. "He duped me."

Cecily stood up from her sewing machine. "Are we talking margarita-level duped or coffee-level duped."

"Coffee," said Megan, flopping down on the couch. "Not that it doesn't deserve margaritas… You know what? Let's make it margaritas."

Cecily headed for the kitchen. "That's my girl. So, what did he do?"

"He almost got me to kiss him."

Cecily turned her head, jaw dropping. "No way."

"Way."

"How'd he do that?"

"He pretended to rescue a wet puppy at the side of the highway."

"A pretend puppy or a puppy he pretended to rescue?"

Megan sniffed at her musty shirt. "It was a real puppy all right. It cuddled up to my stomach all the way home."

Cecily dumped the ice cubes into the blender with a clatter, her face breaking into a grin. "We have a *puppy*?"

"No, Collin has a puppy. I think he planted it out there."

"Planted it out there to make you think he was a nice guy?"

"Yeah."

"You mean to tell me you fell for the old wet-puppy routine?"

"There's a wet-puppy routine?"

Cecily snorted. "Didn't you go to college?"

"Why was I not informed?"

Cecily shrugged, hitting the button on the blender. "You have to keep your ear to the ground on this stuff. I can't be expected to do everything for you."

Megan huffed and sat back, folding her arms across her chest. "Well, don't keep these things a secret in the future."

"I'll try my best." The blender went silent. "But, really, Megan. A guy, whose sole purpose in life is to get you to kiss him, suddenly starts looking like Mr. Benevolent Puppy-Rescuer, and you *don't* get suspicious?"

"We were way up Lookout Mountain Road. It was a pretty elaborate scam."

"Professional soccer players have a staff; they can afford elaborate scams."

"Apparently."

Cecily arrived beside the couch with two full margarita glasses. She handed one to Megan. "You didn't kiss him, right?"

"No. But…"

Cecily's eyebrows went up. "There's a but?"

"There was this reporter skulking in the ditch."

"Right where you found the puppy?"

"Exactly." Megan took a drink. "He got a picture."

Cecily cocked her head sideways. "Puppy aside for a minute, a reporter skulking in the ditch did *not* make you suspicious?"

"I didn't see the reporter until it was too late. To my credit, the minute I saw him, I knew I'd been had."

"So the reporter got a picture of you *not* kissing Collin."

Megan nodded decisively. "Right."

"So what's the problem?"

"I think…on camera…from that angle…I might have looked, kinda, sorta, like I was thinking about it."

Cecily nodded. "Ah-h-h."

"But I won," Megan stated with authority. "Our lips did *not* touch."

"Um-hmm."

"They didn't."

"So why are you so upset?"

Good question. He didn't get the kiss. She was the official winner, with all the bragging rights that went along with it.

Cecily's voice turned sing-song. "Is it because he made you *wan' it*?"

Megan's jaw tensed.

Partly.

Yeah.

The jerk.

She clutched her margarita glass. "Just when I thought…"

Cecily peered over her rim. "Just when you thought what?"

"Just when he was starting to look like a decent human being, what with the puppy and the jacket—"

"The jacket?"

"He gave me his jacket when it started to rain."

"That is decent."

"Part of the act." She never should have fallen for it. And she never would again. It was all behind her now. "Forget Collin," she said decisively. "I met Anna Simpson tonight."

"Who's Anna Simpson?"

"Center forward for the women's Olympic soccer team."

"On your date?"

"It was a strange date. I gave her my card and asked her if she'd be interested in endorsements."

"Good for you. Lemonade out of lemons. What did she say?"

"Nothing."

"Nothing?"

"Collin dragged me away before she could get a word out. Apparently, his puppy was waiting."

"Think she'll call?"

Megan shook her head. "No way to know."

If Anna was in on the puppy scam, she sure wouldn't be calling Megan any time soon. Still, a woman couldn't help but hope.

"That is one suspicious woman," said Collin as he dumped kibble into the new dog dish on the linoleum floor of his kitchen.

Rocky enthusiastically wagged his tail, and Collin took the gesture as agreement, even though the lion's share of the dog's attention was clearly on his breakfast. He nosed his way curiously through the multicolored puppy mix before deciding on a red triangle and crunching it down.

Collin set the box of food on the table and headed for the sink with Rocky's new water dish, carrying on a conversation with the dog as he filled it to the brim. "Didn't score a kiss, but thank God *that* charade is over." He could see the radio station playing it up for a day or so, but after that things would probably calm down.

He wasn't looking forward to the ribbing he'd take from the guys for falling flat on his face. But it wasn't as if he'd expected a kiss. In fact, he was surprised at how close he'd come.

The front doorbell rang. Rocky lifted his head. His floppy ears perked up, and he looked curiously from side to side, obviously trying to locate the source of the sound.

When Collin headed for the door, Rocky immediately abandoned his food dish to accompany him on the mission. The pup definitely had a loyal streak.

Brett stepped right into the house and whapped a folded newspaper against Collin's stomach. "Nice play. Looks like you pulled it out at halftime."

Collin reflexively grabbed for the newspaper before it fell. "Halftime? Pulled what out?" They hadn't played a game yesterday.

The paper came open in Collin's hands. There it was, right square in the middle of the front page, a headshot of him and Megan, leaning in, lips poised, eyes half closed.

It wasn't a particularly good picture of Megan, but Collin felt his stomach clench anyway. The memory of her clinging to his waist, her body pressed flush against his back as they eluded the reporter at eighty miles an hour, was indelibly etched in his brain.

Rocky sat down on the toe of Collin's shoe, staring quizzically at the kitchen door where Brett had disappeared.

When Brett came back with a cup of coffee in his hand, he clapped his other one on Collin's shoulder. "You're the man."

Collin took one last glance at Megan and tossed the paper on the side table of the entry hall. "Came closer than I thought," he said, sorry to have to disappoint Brett.

"Closer to what?"

"To kissing her."

"You didn't kiss her?"

"Nope."

His friend frowned as he retrieved the newspaper.

Curiosity got the better of Rocky's shyness, and he trotted over to sniff Brett's ankles.

"You were within six inches of the woman's lips." Brett flipped the paper around and held it up so the picture was facing Collin. He tapped his index finger on Megan's nose. "And she looked at you like *that*? And you *fumbled* the ball? What is the *matter* with you?"

"I didn't fumble the ball." Collin felt obliged to defend himself. "If it wasn't for that trigger-happy reporter, I'd have easily made first base."

"So, you lost the bet."

Rocky circled Brett's feet, sniffing his shoelace, testing it with his teeth and then hopping back a few feet.

"The bet?" asked Collin.

"I had a twenty riding on you."

"Life sucks sometimes."

Brett finally looked down. "Are you aware of the fact that you have a puppy?"

The doorbell rang a second time.

"Name's Rocky," Collin said as he headed for the door.

Rocky immediately beelined for Collin and trotted at his heel, his chubby belly swaying back and forth with each step on the hardwood floor.

"You didn't have him yesterday," said Brett.

"Found him on my date." Collin opened the door.

Megan was standing on his porch, a broad grin replacing the sour frown she'd left him with last night.

Had he missed something?

"Did you see it?" she asked, brushing past him.

Collin turned and closed the door. "See what?"

"The *newspaper*. We made the front page! You can't buy publicity like that. Not at any price."

"I saw it." Collin sighed, amazed that she wasn't upset. Most women he knew would be ticked off about being caught from that unflattering angle, makeup smeared and wet hair plastered lopsidedly to the side of their head.

Not so Megan. And this morning her curls were sleek and bouncy, caressing her heart-shaped face, accentuating her emerald eyes and coral-pink lips.

Just what Collin needed. An even more beautiful image to replace the bedraggled one in his dreams.

"Isn't it great?" she enthused.

Brett cleared his throat.

Megan abruptly turned toward the sound. "Sorry. Didn't realize you had company."

"Megan Brock, this is Brett Stirling. One of my teammates."

Brett flipped his long hair back and moved forward, offering Megan a wide, white-toothed smile and holding out his hand. "Great to meet you, Megan."

She took his hand. "Brett the Harley owner?"

"That's me."

"In that case…" She smoothly stepped forward, took Brett's face between her hands and planted a long kiss on his lips.

Collin felt his body tense and a wave of cold washed through it. His fists clenched, and it was all he could do not to rip her away.

He took a deep breath and forced himself to stay still.

After a long minute, she pulled back. There was a definite twinkle in her eyes. "Nice bike."

"Nice kiss."

"You two want to get a room?" Collin practically growled.

Rocky whimpered, circling between Collin's legs.

"Unnecessary," said Megan, apparently not fazed by Collin's crude humor. "So, what did you think of the newspaper?"

Collin reached down to pick up the pup.

"We were just checking it out," said Brett.

Megan turned to Collin. "I say we keep a low profile until Tuesday. Then you come back on the show—"

Collin held up one hand, settling Rocky against his chest. "Whoa. Slow down. I'm not coming back on the show."

Her brow creased. "Why not? You can brag about how close you came to kissing me. I can tell everybody you got me soaked and refused to buy my hot dog—"

"You refused to buy her a *hot dog*?" Brett's expression turned incredulous.

"It'll be a hoot," finished Megan.

"This is ending here and now." Collin was still annoyed that she'd kissed Brett so easily, and for no good reason. Sure, she'd made that stupid joke about it last night, but that was a joke. A woman didn't grab a stranger and plant one right on his lips.

"Don't be such a poop." Megan pouted in a way that told Collin she was sure it would work.

"*I'm* not a poop," said Brett. "Why wouldn't you buy her a hot dog?"

Megan ignored him. "It's only an hour-long show. It'll be great for your career."

"Forget it," said Collin.

"I'd go on the show," Brett offered. "And I wouldn't let you go hungry. Maybe you should date me instead."

"I don't think so, Brett." Megan tipped her head and gave him a bright smile. "The kiss wasn't all that good."

"Hey," Brett protested.

Collin grinned, feeling lighter.

"Shut up," Brett said to him. "She didn't even kiss you."

"She would have," said Collin.

"Would not," said Megan.

"Ha. If that reporter hadn't stopped you, you'd have been all over me, babe."

"Wanna tell that to the world?" she asked, brightening.

"Nice try," said Collin.

"You're working on the wrong guy," Brett complained.

Megan shot Collin an exasperated look. "Collin started all this; it's up to him to finish it off."

"I never started this."

"It was you who wanted to be a guest on my show."

"That was Coach."

"Coach likes it when we go for publicity," said Brett. "Good for box-office sales."

"Mercenary," Collin muttered under his breath. Were there no purists left in the sport?

Megan moved a little closer, hitting him with the full force of her jewel-bright eyes and that killer smile. She reached out to stroke her hand along Rocky's stomach, fingertips grazing Collin's chest in the process. "You wouldn't have to do the entire hour," she all but purred.

He steeled himself against her flirtatious fingers.

Rocky, on the other hand, sighed and went limp in ecstasy.

"No dice," said Collin, with all the conviction he could muster.

She took a step closer, still petting the puppy. "How can I sweeten this deal?"

Brett made an inarticulate sound of distress.

Rocky gazed adoringly up at Megan.

"There is nothing you can say or do to make me change my mind," said Collin.

Her shoulders dropped, and her hand fell away from Rocky. "You're such a poop."

Collin gave her a lopsided grin and took over, scratching behind Rocky's ears. "I guess life just plain sucks some days."

She straightened a little. "It doesn't have to. You could make it not suck today."

"I am fundamentally opposed to the commercialization of athletes."

"See, there's where you're misguided."

"I'm not misguided."

"You're clinging to an outdated principle."

"Principles don't go out of date."

"Adapt or perish."

"Perish?"

"Law of the jungle, baby."

"I'm a soccer player, not a gazelle."

She pursed her lips, obviously struggling to come up with another approach.

He tried not to think about kissing them, about how

Brett had kissed them, about how badly he wanted equal time.

A gleam came into her eyes, and she opened her mouth again.

"You won't win," he quickly warned her.

She closed her mouth, and her eyes narrowed speculatively. To his surprise, she took a couple of backward steps toward the door.

He couldn't help but grin at her defiant expression. It was definitely a tactical retreat, not a surrender.

She rested her hand on the knob while sizing him up. "This may take a little time."

By Sunday afternoon, Megan had conceived and discarded a dozen plans for getting Collin to do Tuesday's show.

Dressed in her oldest sweatpants, she sat sprawled on her couch, her feet propped up on the coffee table and a huge bowl of popcorn balanced in her lap. She was channel surfing while postponing a trip to the Laundromat. If she was lucky, she'd find a rare old movie and have an excuse to put her life on hold for a few hours.

Game show, horror movie, sitcom…

She scooped a handful of popcorn and plunked the crisp kernels one at a time into her mouth, enjoying the little squeak on her teeth as she chewed. Her water glass was empty, but the ice cubes had melted a little, so she trickled the cold fragments down her throat.

Evangelist, rap music, cooking show, soccer game…

Wait a minute.

She flipped back.

It was the Denver Peaks. And there was Collin. Large as life on her television screen, looking steadfast and sweaty and sexy. He sprinted down the field, dribbling along the sideline before passing the ball and shouting an instruction to a teammate.

Holy cow. The teammate was Brett.

Megan couldn't help but grin at seeing them in action on her television screen after talking to them just yesterday.

A referee blew the whistle. The action stopped, and the camera panned back. It showed a cluster of yelling fans in the bleachers, a row of green jerseys on the bench, and two men in black windbreakers standing by the sidelines.

Must be the coach.

She sat up straight, sliding the popcorn bowl onto the coffee table as Brett's words echoed in her mind. *Coach likes it when we go for publicity.*

"Is this live?" she asked the empty room anxiously, leaning toward the screen, turning the volume.

A banner flashed on the top. Live from Denver—the Peaks versus United.

Megan gasped her excitement. Popcorn crumbs fell off her chest as she reached for the phone, dialing the radio station.

Brett had definitely said the coach liked publicity. If she could get there before the end of the game, maybe the man would help her convince Collin to appear on the show.

The radio station switchboard picked up.

"Roland Scavolini," Megan said breathlessly, twisting the phone cord with impatience.

"Scavolini here."

"Roland? It's Megan."

"Hiya, Megan."

"Any chance I could get a sound crew to meet me at the stadium?"

There was a silent pause. "A sound crew?"

"Yeah. I want to go remote."

Another silence. "You want to *go remote?*"

"Roland."

"Megan. What are you talking about? Phone-in shows don't go remote, *reporters* go remote. You know, when there's *news* out there."

"I want to talk to Collin at the stadium."

"Why? Have they taken hostages at the stadium?"

"I think I might be able to get him on the air."

"How?"

"It's hard to explain. But we've gotta move. There's no time to mess around."

"I can't do that, Megan."

"Then who can?"

"The station manager."

"Ask him."

"He's not here."

"Who's in charge?"

"I am."

"*Well…*"

"Do you have any idea how much trouble I could get into over something like that?"

"You have any idea how high we could boost our ratings with something like that?"

"Easy for you to say; it's not your ass on the line."

"Isn't it? I was the one in the newspaper. I'm the one who's going on the air on Tuesday. I figure half my audience, *your* listeners, are going to be expecting him too—"

"For God's sake, Megan."

"Don't be a wuss. Take chances, make mistakes—"

"Fine," Roland snapped. "But don't you dare leave that stadium until you *get* him signed on."

"I won't." She wouldn't. Definitely. She hoped.

"I'll send Arnold with a couple of press passes."

Megan clenched her fist and shut her eyes. "Yes!"

"This is on your head."

"Right."

"You screw up, and there won't *be* a Perfect Boyfriend show on Tuesday."

Megan stood in the tunnel that led from the stadium to the locker rooms, microphone in her hand, a fine sheet of sweat forming on her brow. Arnold hovered behind her, checking switches on the remote transmitter while she received the occasional message from Roland back at the station through her headset.

Megan couldn't see the game, but she could hear the shouts of the crowd and watch the scoreboard timer as it counted the minutes. There hadn't been time to track Cecily down and tell her about the plan, so Megan was risking it all on her own.

She flipped back her hair, straightening the navy blazer she'd borrowed from Cecily's closet.

The whistle sounded three times, and the home crowd roared over the two-one win.

Megan squared her shoulders, backing up against the concrete wall as a flood of players streamed past.

"There he is," she said to Arnold, moving into the fray.

"We're putting you on," said Roland into her earpiece.

"Mr. O'Patrick," she called against the noise of the crowd and the players' exchange of congratulatory remarks and high fives. She ducked between bodies, hoping Arnold could keep up.

She moved in right beside Collin. "Megan Brock, KNOA radio forty-five."

He gave her an incredulous look. "I know who you are."

"Congratulations on the win."

"Thanks," he grunted, increasing his speed down the corridor.

Megan had to practically jog to keep up. "We're live on KNOA, and the listeners are wondering if you have any comments on your *perfect* date from Friday night."

Collin stared at her as if she'd grown two heads. He didn't say a word, just bashed the flat of his hand against the locker-room door, swinging it open. He shook his head, and disappeared inside.

Megan's stomach bottomed out. She'd thought he'd say something, fight with her, argue with her, *something*.

She glanced around, hoping to see the coach.

The corridor was emptying.

Everybody was in the locker room.

"We broke to commercial," came Roland's voice. "Get something, Megan."

Megan glanced at Arnold, then glanced at the locker-room door.

Arnold grinned and shrugged.

Megan took a deep breath. She wouldn't be the first woman reporter to storm the bastion of the men's locker room. Surely to goodness the showers weren't front and center.

She pushed open the door.

The locker room was a crowded mass of sweaty male chests, whoops and grunts, shower steam and oppressive heat.

Megan peered through the crowd, spotting Collin and Brett at the end of the long bench. She elbowed her way toward him.

"Mr. O'Patrick." She shoved the microphone in his face. "Is the reason you failed on the date because The Perfect Boyfriend list is right and you were wrong?"

"Hey, Megan," said Brett with a broad grin and a wink in her direction. "Got any questions for me?"

Megan smiled back at him. He seemed like a nice guy, but their kiss had been chaste and flat. She knew it. He knew it. The flirting was all for show.

"Are you ready to admit defeat to the world?" she asked Collin.

Instead of answering, he bent down to unlace his soccer shoes, remaining defiantly silent.

"Megan," Roland growled in her ear.

She struggled to get a rise out of Collin. "Is that a yes?"

Still nothing.

"Well, Denver," Megan prattled on, desperate to fill

the dead air space. "Megan Brock coming to you live from the Denver Peaks' locker room where they've just come off a win against Miami United and we're trying to talk to Collin O'Patrick about why he's not the perfect boyfriend. But, I have to tell you, Denver, it looks to me like Collin has something to hide."

He straightened, and she moved a little closer.

"Why do you suppose you didn't get a kiss, Collin? Was it the ambience? Your technique? Are you willing to admit a few of the items on the list might have helped? Like maybe flowers? Dinner? Civility?"

She thrust the microphone back at him, starting to get annoyed. "Well, he's not answering us, Denver. Maybe his mother didn't teach him any manners. Or maybe he can't do two things at once. I can tell you he's spent the past two minutes unlacing his shoes. Oh, he's taking them off now. Probably can't walk and chew gum, either."

Brett chuckled.

"Can you talk yet, Collin?" she asked. "Guess not. Oh, he's moving on to the shirt. Stripping it off." She inhaled sharply. "Don't know how many of you have seen Collin O'Patrick without his shirt on, but, I gotta tell you, it's worth the price of admission."

"Excuse me, ma'am," came an officious voice from behind her.

Oh, great. Now Security was going to kick her out. Her radio career was over before it had had a chance to begin.

Before anyone touched her, Brett's voice broke in. "Coach, it's *her*."

"Nice pecs," said Megan, unable to think of anything

else. "Broad shoulders, doesn't have a hairy chest. Well, I'll be, that gives him something on my list, doesn't it? Who'd've guessed?"

"Her who?" asked the coach in the background.

"Her, Perfect Boyfriend Megan Brock, that's who," said Brett.

Collin crossed his arms and pasted her with a look of absolute disgust.

Megan stared straight into his slate-gray eyes. "Great biceps, too."

"Carry on," said the coach in an undertone.

"Still not ready to make a comment, Mr. O'Patrick?"

His mouth curved up in a cool half-smile and he reached for the waistband of his shorts.

Didn't he know not to play chicken with the woman holding the microphone? The one whose job was on the line?

"He's going for the shorts," said Megan. "Maybe once he's naked we can get a word out of him."

Collin pulled off his shorts and stood there in nothing but his briefs.

The entire locker room was silent. Collin's coach and his teammates gathered around, obviously as curious as Megan to see how far this would go.

She had to admit, she was getting a little nervous. What the hell was she going to do if he stripped off his Jockeys? Did she honestly think she could stand here and taunt a naked man on live radio?

"Nice legs," she said into the microphone, her voice coming through a little dry and breathless. She felt like that first night on air, jittery with anticipation, excited and giddy and nervous all at the same time—hoping against hope that her vocal cords would hold out and her brain wouldn't go blank.

"If you turn around, I can give the greater Denver area a nice description of your butt. Unless you'd like to make some comment on our date instead?"

Unexpectedly, Collin took a step toward her.

Megan drew back in surprise, but quickly recovered. "Something to say?"

Suddenly his arm went around her, pressing solid against the small of her back.

Her microphone hand dropped to her side, and she bent slightly backward, off balance.

He followed her. "Describe this to the listening audience," he growled.

Somebody scooped up the microphone before it could clatter to the floor.

Collin's lips met hers and his almost-naked body pressed tight against her from head to toe.

His lips were warm, firm, and just moist enough to be interesting.

Her hands went to his slick shoulders, trying to steady herself.

His skin was like fire, burning an electrical pathway along her arms. Something jolted inside her, and all of her senses tuned to his mouth.

His lips softened, parted further, turning this from playacting to a real kiss. The arm across her back tightened, and his other hand tunneled its way into her hair.

Megan felt her body go limp. She opened for him, marveling at the sensations zipping around her body, awakening desires that seemed to have slumbered forever.

"Interesting turn of events, folks," Brett's musical voice intruded from the background. "Looks like O'Patrick finally got his kiss."

A cheer went up from the watching players.

Megan prayed the floor would open up and swallow her whole.

She forced herself to pull back, and Collin loosened his hold.

As he straightened them both he whispered harshly against her ear, "Don't you *ever* take me on again."

It was meant as a warning, but all Megan could think about was how much she'd like to take Collin on again.

CHAPTER SIX

COLLIN *hated* that he was making a spectacle of himself—particularly in front of his teammates. He also hated that such an annoying woman could be such a fantastic kisser. If she'd planted one like that on Brett, no wonder the guy didn't want to take no for an answer.

Collin put Megan firmly away from him, hoping she was embarrassed, and she would back the hell off. He wanted nothing more than to put this humiliating episode behind him.

Megan took a step backward, breathing deeply—the determined light gone from her eyes. She looked confused for a second, then she blinked her way to recovery and her green eyes smoldered with annoyance.

Next to them, Brett still held the microphone. "Tell us, Coach," he said in a hearty voice, "on a scale of one to ten, how would you rate that kiss?"

To Collin's astonishment, Coach chimed right in.

"I'd have to give it a six, Stirling. And, for my money, the lady was willing."

Megan miraculously recovered her voice. "I wasn't *willing*," she sputtered.

"Looked willing to me," said Brett. Then he nodded to the team. "What about you guys? You think she was willing?"

The players cheered in support of Collin.

He couldn't help grinning with a level of satisfaction. See how *Megan* liked being the butt of Denver's joke.

"Optical illusion," she claimed.

Brett spoke up again, a distinctly evil gleam in his eyes. "Question now, Coach, is how do we break the tie?"

Damn it, Collin cussed himself. It didn't take a rocket scientist to see where this was going. He lunged for the microphone, but Brett deftly side-stepped him.

The problem with soccer honing his reflexes to that of a jungle cat's was that his entire team ended up with the same reflexes.

"Collin should come back on the show," Megan quickly suggested, her voice loud and commanding as she leaned toward the mike. Funny how a woman could go from stunned silence to mercenary scheming in the blink of an eye.

He should probably take it as a compliment that he'd managed to shut her up for any time at all.

"Collin would love to be a guest on the show again," said Coach.

Brett drew back. "How does that settle—?"

Coach grabbed the microphone before he could finish the question.

"Tuesday night?" Coach asked Megan.

"Tuesday night at nine," she confirmed.

"I'm going to get you for this," Collin muttered in her ear.

"Hold that thought until Tuesday," she whispered back. Then she looked him up and down. "In the meantime, you might consider getting dressed."

"I'm getting into the shower. You want to share the intimate details of my butt with your audience? Stick around."

"You wouldn't."

Collin hooked his thumbs into the waistband of his Jockeys, completely willing to get naked if that was what it took to get her out of there.

Megan's green eyes went wide. She scooped the microphone out of Coach's hand.

"That's a wrap," she said into it, heading for the locker-room door, signaling for her sound man to follow.

"Thanks for joining us here in the Denver Peaks' locker room," she continued, "for our interview following their big win over Miami United. This is Megan Brock reporting for KNOA radio forty-five. Don't forget to tune in Tuesday night at nine o'clock for The Perfect Boyfriend show, where our special guest will be soccer star, Collin O'Patrick."

And then she was gone.

Collin stripped off his underwear, ignoring the commentary from the team as he headed for the showers. There *had* to be a way out of this nightmare.

* * *

It was only Monday, but Megan's week just kept getting better and better. Collin was coming back on the show. Roland was thrilled with the success of the live remote and impressed at the way she had turned near disaster into a ratings grab. One of her biggest advertising clients, Ferretti Industries, had given the thumbs-up on a new baby-food campaign. And now she'd just looked up to see Anna Simpson walk into the outer office.

Megan quickly straightened away from her receptionist's desk. "Anna. So great to see you again."

Anna closed the hallway door behind her, looking a little self-conscious. "Do you have time to talk?" she asked.

"Of course." Megan handed her receptionist the pen she'd borrowed. "Jennifer, can you get the drawings to the courier by two?"

"No problem."

"Thanks." Megan turned back to smile warmly at Anna. "Come on into my office."

It wasn't the biggest or the classiest office in the world, but Megan was proud of the fact that she'd gone from a two-person business to a four-person business in less than two years. She liked the classic ambience of the historical building. And who could beat having an office at street level and an apartment above?

She gestured to one of the padded chairs that surrounded her small meeting table as she closed the door behind them. "Please make yourself comfortable."

Anna sat down, and Megan took the chair across from her, trying not to let her excitement show. She wasn't exactly starstruck, but she very much admired Anna's achievements, and she'd love nothing better than to add the soccer player to her list of clients.

Anna took a breath. "I was wondering if you were serious?" she asked.

"Serious?"

"About getting me some commercials."

Megan straightened, her pulse taking a jump. "Of *course* I was serious. I'd be thrilled to try and make a deal for you."

"It's not so much the money for me," said Anna, her fingertips tracing small patterns of the tabletop. "My training and travel expenses are covered. It's the Panthers. We could really use some extra money for out-of-state tournaments."

"The Panthers. Your soccer team?" asked Megan.

Anna nodded.

Megan's brain started to work on potential angles. "Do you think some of the girls might be interested in participating?"

Anna's brows rose. "In making commercials?"

Megan nodded. She had the beginnings of an idea that Ferretti Industries might just go for.

Anna coughed out a chopped laugh. "They'd be thrilled to the tips of their cleats."

Megan's intercom buzzed.

"Sorry." She rose from her chair, wondering what could be important enough that Jennifer would interrupt the meeting.

She leaned across her desk and pressed the button. "Yes?"

"Collin O'Patrick to see you."

"Here?"

"Yes."

Megan cringed. He was going to try to get out of tomorrow's show. No doubt about it.

"I don't mind if he joins us," said Anna.

Of course she didn't. They were friends, after all. Megan just hoped that didn't mean they'd gang up on her.

"Send him in," she said to Jennifer.

Before Megan could straighten toward the door, it burst open.

"Are *you* responsible for this?" Collin boomed. He waved a newspaper in front of her face.

"Hi, Collin," Anna chirped.

Collin turned to blink at her, an incredulous expression coming over his face.

"Responsible for what?" Megan whisked the paper from his hand.

"What are *you* doing here?" Collin asked Anna.

"Talking to Megan…one heck of a lot more politely than you are, I might add."

Collin scowled. "Your being here is a bad idea, Anna."

Megan smirked. Guess they weren't ganging up after all. She glanced down at the paper. It was folded open to reveal a full-page ad about tomorrow night's Perfect Boyfriend show—which, apparently, was being shot on location at the Sangre Mall.

Tickets were free, and the public was encouraged to attend.

Hoo boy. No wonder Collin was pissed.

The telephone on her desk rang, which meant Jennifer had seen fit to interrupt yet again. Who now?

Megan picked up the receiver. "Megan Brock."

"Megan, it's Roland. I tried to call earlier. The brass gave me an order."

"So I see."

"You see?"

"I'm looking at the newspaper right now." She glanced at Collin, hoping he was getting that she hadn't known about this in advance. Not that she thought it was a bad idea. In fact, she thought it was a terrific idea, but she wouldn't have deliberately hidden it from him.

"Can you be at the mall an hour early?" Roland asked.

"No problem," Megan agreed easily. This was big. Really big. The exposure they'd get from a live remote with an audience was priceless.

"Is Cecily working at Well Suited today?"

"She is."

"I'll call her there."

"Sounds good. Thanks, Roland."

"Thank *you*. You've given the guys down in marketing their thrill of the month."

"Happy to help out. See you tomorrow."

She hung up the phone and looked Collin straight in the eye. "So, what's got the burr up your butt?"

His complexion went a shade darker. "Every time I turn around, this damn thing gets bigger and bigger."

"So?" Bigger was just fine by Megan.

His tone turned staccato and demanding. "I want out."

Megan shrugged. "So, quit."

The cavalier dare was a risk on her part. But logic told her if he'd been planning to up and quit, he'd have done it without telling her. The fact that he was here meant he needed a verbal punching bag before he capitulated.

Well, she wasn't anybody's verbal punching bag.

"And go against my coach's orders?" he asked.

Megan held up her hands in a gesture of confusion. "You're a big boy."

"And I happen to be a professional. That means I listen to my coach."

"And *I* happen to be a professional. That means I listen to my producer."

"At least tell him you want to do it from the studio."

"To please you?"

"Yes!"

"Listen, Collin. Roland tells me to show up at the mall in a purple hat with my face painted green, I say 'sure'."

He paused for a tense moment. "You have zero standards."

"Don't you get all sanctimonious on me—"

"You're a slave to your ratings."

"*You're* a slave to your unbending, steel trap of a mind that a new idea couldn't open with a crowbar."

Collin sucked in a sharp breath, obviously getting ready to rebut, when the office door opened behind him.

Megan glanced past his broad chest to see Brett standing in the doorway.

"You guys know you can hear *everything* you say out there?" He whisked the door shut behind him.

Megan felt her face heat.

Brett spotted Anna at the table. His jaw went tight. "Anna," he said with a slight nod.

Anna gave him a cool acknowledgement in return. "Brett."

Megan glanced from one to the other, trying to gauge the current running between then. Then she looked back at Collin and decided the current coming from *him* was the one to worry about.

Brett glanced at his watch. "We gotta move it," he said to Collin.

"She won't do it." Collin shifted toward the door.

"Of course she won't do it," said Brett. "She'd be a fool."

"Excuse me," snapped Megan. "I am in the room."

"And, for my money, you're one savvy woman," said Brett. "Sorry we have to take off. We've got practice."

"Hey, Anna," said Collin, with what looked like a flash of inspiration. "You want to join us?"

Anna drew back, eyebrows going up. "Me? At the stadium?"

Brett hit Collin with an astonished glare.

Megan ignored the lurch in her stomach at the invitation. It wasn't jealousy. Collin was nothing but a pain. If he had a thing for Anna, it was no skin off her nose.

"Sure," said Collin. "If you don't mind watching for a while, we can kick the ball around after. Right, Brett?"

Brett was silent, still staring at Collin for a minute as if he'd lost his mind. "Yeah. Sure. Why not?"

"Megan and I were just about to…" Anna glanced at Megan, clearly dying to accept what was obviously an unusual offer.

Megan took in Collin's uneasy expression. It was as if a lot rested on Anna's answer.

Did he have a thing for her? Was this some kind of date? He'd never struck Megan as the bashful type, so why would he go all junior high now?

Either he had a schoolboy crush on Anna, or he was dangling the bribe of soccer practice to get her away from Megan's evil, mercenary influence.

Bingo.

Nice try, baby.

She was stopping this in its tracks.

"Why don't I come, too?" she put in brightly before Anna had a chance to respond. "Anna and I can talk while we watch."

"Great idea," agreed Anna.

Collin's forehead creased.

Megan cocked her head in his direction, unable to resist a triumphant smirk that would tell him she had his number.

Sitting in the first row of the stadium stands, Megan quickly got all the information she needed from Anna. Just as well that they both talked fast, since several of the players stopped by between drills to chat. Most of them appeared to have heard of Anna, if not met her, and all were respectful of her talent and skill.

The conversations moved into technical soccer talk, and Megan found her gaze resting on Collin out in the field. She knew she should grab a cab and head back to the office now that she'd finished with Anna, but she kept promising herself just two more minutes of soccer voyeurism.

When he wasn't arguing with her or glaring at her, she had to admit, Collin was gorgeous.

He wore a pair of loose shorts that rode low on his hips and a cropped tank top that showed off his washboard stomach and powerful shoulders. As the practice wore on a sheen of sweat formed on his body and his hair went a shade darker with dampness. And his total intensity and focus on the game was, for some reason, dangerously sexy.

She knew she was crazy to fantasize about him. But she couldn't help remembering the sensation of his sweaty kiss, the feel of his strong arms around her, the hormonal rush that had crested through her body like a tidal wave. And that had been in front of thirty witnesses. She tried to imagine how she'd react to a kiss from Collin in private.

It could be fantastic.

It could be phenomenal.

Maybe after this radio challenge was all over she should come up with an excuse to give it a try.

What could it hurt? They were both adults. They were under no illusions about their feelings for one another. It would be sexual attraction, pure and simple.

The practice turned to a scrimmage, and Collin faced

off at center with another player. He captured the ball and sprinted the length of the field, his muscular thighs carrying him like the wind as he kept it safe between his feet, dodging around the defenders, heading for the goal.

He got clear in right field, passing it to Brett, who was immediately covered by two opposing players.

Brett chipped it over their heads back to Collin, who leaped up and kicked it in midair, landing sprawled on the ground as the ball sailed over the goalie's head and into the top corner of the net.

Megan practically jumped out of her seat.

"Nice goal," said Anna from beside her.

Nice man, thought Megan. He jumped up, his wide grin crinkling the corners of his eyes and showing off straight white teeth as he accepted the congratulations of his teammates. If he ever decided to go commercial, he'd have sponsors begging him to endorse their products.

Forget selling to men, he'd have millions of women all over the world buying his number jersey just to sleep in it.

While the players set up at center field, Brett glanced over to the bench for about the twentieth time. For some reason, he'd seemed inordinately interested in the parade of players dropping by to chat. He kept looking distracted by the activity, almost annoyed.

Curious, Megan turned her attention to Anna's profile.

Her face was animated as she talked with Marc Allendale, one of the players. She was a beautiful woman, healthy, fresh-faced, barely a speck of makeup. Megan could see how a man would be attracted to tanned skin and barely discernible freckles.

Marc rolled to his feet. "I'm up next," he apologized with a smile and a wave.

Had Marc been flirting? Perhaps making Brett jealous? Megan had been so focused on Collin that she had no way of knowing.

"So, what's the deal with you and Brett?" she asked Anna.

Anna turned her head, drawing back. "Me and Brett?"

"Yeah. You know him, right?"

"Uh huh. Known him since college. He's a boor."

"Really? I thought he seemed pretty nice."

Anna frowned, her attention straying to the field. "He's loud, brash and full of himself."

"But good-looking and kinda hot."

"And doesn't he *know* it."

"He ever make a move?"

"On who?"

"On you."

Anna shook her head, chuckling dryly. "More than his sorry little life is worth."

"So, you don't want him to?"

"Of course not."

There was a silent pause while Megan waited to see if Anna was going to elaborate. The shouts of the players and the coach's whistle penetrated.

"Why?" asked Anna.

"I don't know. Back at my office, I thought I sensed something…" Megan shook her head. "I don't know."

"He's not my type," said Anna. "And he'd *never* make your list."

Megan chuckled. "No blender drinks?"

"No blender drinks. I doubt he has a clue where there's a single florist in the greater Denver area. And when he's not 'out with the guys' he's with some airhead Barbie doll who'll laugh at *his* jokes."

"He's definitely interested in your career," Megan pointed out.

"No. He's interested in *his* career. He couldn't care less about mine."

Megan smiled, finding Anna's knee-jerk, reaction very interesting, especially when juxtaposed with Brett's apparent jealousy of the men who'd been stopping by to chat. Of course, she wasn't about to tell Anna that.

"Definitely not your type," she said instead.

"Not if he was the last man on earth," Anna nodded.

The coach blew a long, shrill blast on the whistle, which apparently signaled the end of practice. The players all jogged to the sideline, grabbing towels and helping themselves to cups of water and bottled sports drinks.

Brett lingered on the field, while Collin trotted over to Anna and Megan.

"Ready to play?" he asked Anna.

She jumped up. "Let's go."

Collin tossed her the ball, and she trapped it under one foot before dribbling her way onto the field.

He turned to Megan, a gleam in his eye. "You, too."

Megan's stomach jumped. "I don't play soccer."

"We'll take it easy on you."

She shook her head. "No way."

"You're wearing sneakers."

"I don't do soccer." It had been nearly ten years since she'd played any kind of a team sport.

He reached for her hand. "I gotta play in your arena. Then you gotta play in mine."

"*Collin.*"

He tugged on her hand. "I'm not asking, Megan. I'm telling."

"Take a hike."

"Kick a ball."

"My favorite, and *only* form of exercise is dancing."

His grip tightened, and he pulled her to her feet. "Fine. We'll go dancing after we finish playing soccer."

"I was—"

"Fair's fair."

Megan stumbled into a walk, glancing at the players who'd begun paying attention to the exchange. "I'm going to look like a fool," she snapped.

"Welcome to the club, babe."

They passed the cluster of soccer players in silence.

"You recognize those guys back there?" asked Collin, jerking his head as he pulled her out of hearing range.

"Some of them." She hated to admit it, but his big, warm hand was starting to feel kind of good. Why, oh, why couldn't it come packaged with a nice guy?

"Well, all those players watched you make a fool of me in my underwear yesterday."

"They also watched you kiss me in your underwear and *win* the contest."

His grip loosened, but he didn't let go of her hand. "Thought you said you weren't willing?"

She gazed up at him. "You were there."

"You're conceding?"

"You know I kissed you back. Of course, I'll lie through my teeth about it on the air tomorrow."

His voice rose. "See what I have to put up with? I'm on display in my freakin' underwear, in front of my entire team, while you practically have microphone sex with me over the radio waves, and my coach signs me up for another evening in purgatory, and you won't even admit I won. You owe me for that, Ms. Brock."

A tingle started where their hands were joined, spiraling its way up her body and racing through her extremities. "Owe you what?"

"I haven't decided yet."

"Well, keep me posted."

They drew closer to where Brett and Anna were having one of those soccer ball trick contests.

He dropped his voice. "Maybe you should kiss me in *your* underwear."

Oh, man. There went the tingle again. "In front of your team?"

Collin coughed out a laugh. "I don't think so."

Were they flirting? Megan couldn't tell. Just in case, she let her voice go bedroom husky. "If not in front of the team, where do you want me, then?"

He stopped and turned to face her, staring pointedly into her eyes. "Do you always play with fire?"

She let a beat of silence go by. "Not always."

"I just got lucky?"

"I suppose that depends on the underwear, now, doesn't it?"

Collin swore under his breath, his Irish accent thicker than usual. "Don't be doing this, Megan."

"Don't be doing what?"

"Don't be messing with my head."

"I'm flirting with you, Collin." She blinked her lashes. "You know…making promises I only half intend to keep. Surely it's happened to you before."

"You actually *half intend* to kiss me in your underwear?"

"I suppose you'll have to wait to find that out, won't you?"

"Hey, O'Patrick," came Brett's voice from twenty feet away. "Let go of the woman and get the ball."

Collin stared at Megan a split second longer, confusion mixed with fascination as the black and white ball sailed past them.

She'd happily take his fascination. *She* was growing more fascinated by the minute—with no way of knowing where it was heading.

They had to get through Tuesday before anything remotely sexual could happen between them. But, for now, his confusion was totally gratifying.

In fact, she'd like to keep him that way for a while. With an enigmatic smile, she slowly drew her hand away from his and headed for Brett and Anna.

CHAPTER SEVEN

COLLIN hadn't realized Megan was serious about dancing. Yet here she was, gyrating in front of him on the dance floor of Addison's. Lights flashed with the heavy beat as a surprisingly full Monday-night crowd soaked up the sounds of classic rock from the club band on stage.

He and Brett were wearing jeans and T-shirts. Megan and Anna were more formal in slacks and blouses, but Megan had turfed her blazer and pushed up the sleeves of her, blue pinstriped blouse. The contrasting white collar and cuffs set off her light tan, and her blonde curls had grown more wild as the evening had worn on.

When she put her arms over her head, a narrow band of tanned stomach peaked out from her low-riding pants. She looked like a renegade beach bunny at the end of a long, hot day.

Collin felt a jolt of desire—the third one in as many minutes. She might be opinionated and abrasive, but she was also sexy as sin.

The song changed; the rhythm slowed.

Megan smiled, moving toward him with catlike grace, her arms still twining sinuously above her head. She wrapped them around his neck and slid gracefully into the new beat.

He quickly recovered from his surprise that she was willing to slow-dance and slid his arms around her waist, deliberately letting the movements of the dance work her blouse up higher, so he could press his bare forearm against her silky, heated skin. He let his cheek rest against her soft hair.

"You're better at this than you are at soccer," he muttered against her ear.

"That's not saying much," she responded, obviously reliving her turn in goal. "The fetal position isn't my best angle."

He chuckled low at the memory. "We wouldn't have hit you, you know."

"Projectiles the size of my head were whizzing past me at ninety miles an hour. Only a moron wouldn't have taken cover."

"Well, as a soccer player, you make a great dancer."

There was an impish smile in her voice. "And as a dancer, you make a great soccer player."

"Ouch."

"Hey, we have to take the good with the bad."

He let his cheek shift until it was rubbing gently against hers. She smelled of wild flowers and fresh air, felt soft as the spring rain on a Killarney hillside. "I have to admit, this is the most fun I've ever had being insulted."

"Glad to be of service," she whispered.

Her hips brushed his, once, then twice, fleetingly, then longer.

He gritted his teeth against the heady sensation of her body, the rounded curves molding to him like sun-warmed butter. Unless he was completely screwing up the signals, she was as attracted to him as he was to her.

His thoughts moved to how she'd taste after the tart, cranberry martini, and whether her red lips were as soft as her cheeks. He thought they were, but memories could be deceiving, particularly since he hadn't been able to give yesterday's kiss his full attention.

He turned his head slightly, letting his lips follow the line of her jaw.

"Collin," she warned.

"What?"

"No kissing."

"Oh. Yeah. Kissing." Serious kissing.

"Not tonight."

He flicked his tongue out to taste her salty skin. "What's that supposed to mean?"

"We're on the air tomorrow, remember?"

"You're already planning to lie."

"Somebody could see us."

"But I thought—"

"You thought I brought you dancing so we could make out?"

Collin glanced down to where their bodies touched, full-frontal touching. "You're plastered against me like green on a shamrock."

"It's all for show."

"Show to who?"

She tipped her head, motioning across the dance floor.

Collin looked over at the other couples. "What? There a reporter out there you're trying to tease?"

"No." She cocked her head again.

"What?"

"Them."

"Them who?"

"Them Brett and Anna."

Collin searched for the logic in her statement. "You brought me dancing so we could fool Brett and Anna into thinking we had the hots for each other?"

Megan pulled back. "I brought you dancing so *they'd* come dancing."

"And?"

"I'm matchmaking *them*, not us."

"Them?"

"Them."

"You're nuts, you know that? Brett and Anna have known each other for five years. She was a freshman while he was a junior at State."

"And they haven't gotten together yet?"

"Why would they get together? They don't even like each other."

"Sure they do."

"They argue all the time."

"You mean they have emotional reactions to each other all the time."

"No. I mean they argue."

He stared at Brett and Anna while they danced. It was obvious from the fire in their eyes and the speed of Anna's lips that they were having another one of their famous arguments.

"I think there's more to it than that," said Megan.

"Whatever," said Collin. "I want to get back to us."

"There is no us."

"Us." He rocked a finger back and forth between their chests. "After the radio show tomorrow. Somewhere private. I pick the underwear."

He knew she'd refuse. But he wanted to get a rise out of her.

"I said I only *half* intended to kiss you in my underwear."

He shrugged. "So only wear half your underwear."

Before she had a chance to answer, the band ended the song on a long note and the lead singer thanked the audience.

The final set was over, and the moment was gone.

Collin led Megan from the dance floor, squelching his disappointment. He wasn't getting a kiss tonight, and that was that. He might not know Megan well, but her stubborn streak was the first thing he'd learned about her.

When they got to the table, Anna was laughing as Brett helped her into her sweater and she downed the last of her martini.

"Whew. I'm definitely not driving back up Lookout Mountain Road tonight."

Hands on her shoulders, Brett opened his mouth to speak.

"Stay at my place," Megan interrupted, cutting off whatever it was Brett had been about to say. She lifted her blazer from the back of her chair. "I've got a fold-out couch."

A fleeting expression crossed Brett's face, and Collin tried to place it.

"You sure?" Anna asked Megan.

"We can grab the shuttle," said Megan.

"I'll drop you off," Brett said with a scowl.

Obviously hearing something in his voice, Anna craned her neck to look up at him. "We don't want to put you to any trouble, grumpy-pants."

"No trouble."

"Sure it's not."

"I said it's no trouble."

Megan gave Collin a look that said she'd told him so.

He moved toward her, pretending to help with her blazer. "It's an argument," he muttered.

"It's foreplay," she whispered back.

"You're warped."

"I'm right."

"So what is it you and I are doing?"

She paused for half a beat. "I don't think we've figured that out yet."

"Sleepy?" Megan asked Anna as they crossed the foyer to her apartment.

"Jazzed," said Anna.

Megan was feeling a little jazzed herself. "Because you had fun dancing?"

"Because I don't usually drink martinis on Monday nights." Anna put a hand against the wall to steady herself.

Megan paused with keys in hand. She didn't usually drink on Monday nights either, but, now that she had the buzz going, it seemed a shame to cut it short. "You have to work in the morning?"

"Nope. You?"

"I'm the boss." Megan grinned. Though mostly that status meant she started early and worked late, there was nothing wrong with taking advantage every so often.

She took a step back from her apartment door and crooked her finger at Anna. "This way," she sang, crossing the foyer to Cecily's door.

"Where we going?" asked Anna.

"Cecily's apartment. Guaranteed to have margarita fixin's twenty-four-seven."

Anna's eyes widened in the dim light. "We're breaking in to steal margaritas?"

Megan jingled her key chain in front of Anna's nose. "I have the key."

"So, we're *letting* ourselves in to steal margaritas."

"Exactly."

"Won't we wake her up?"

Megan peeled off her shoes, and put her index finger across her lips. "We'll be quiet."

Anna slipped off her own shoes. "Quiet?" she staged whispered. "While *making margaritas*?"

Megan carefully slipped the key in the lock, whispering back, "Yeah. I suppose the blender might be a problem. We'll take it all to my place."

Megan turned the handle and gently pushed the door open. The hinges made a long, low squeak.

"Shh," said Anna.

"I'm trying."

Light from the street filtered through the front window, outlining the furniture in black, and giving the curtains a ghostly gray glow. She clicked the door shut behind her. "Follow me. The kitchen's this way."

Anna stuck close to her back as they padded across the living room into the tiny kitchen. Once Megan opened the fridge and the light blinked on, it was relatively easy to see what they were doing. She located limes in the produce drawer, then liberated a bottle of tequila from Cecily's liquor cabinet.

The blender was more of a problem. For one thing, it was disassembled, and the seal, lid and blades were strewn around the counter.

Megan handed Anna the glass pitcher, then gathered up the smaller pieces, dumping the fistful into the pitcher. They immediately clattered to the floor.

She let out a little shriek. "You didn't put your hand *over the bottom*?"

Anna sputtered out a laugh. "Sorry. Forgot about that part."

Megan fought back her own giggle, dropping down on all fours to retrieve the parts.

A light suddenly flooded the room.

"*What* are you doing?" mumbled Cecily from the bedroom doorway, pushing her messy hair back from her forehead, adjusting the man's dress shirt she wore as a nightgown.

"You got a guy in there?" asked Megan.

Cecily's face scrunched up. "No."

"What's with the shirt?"

Cecily looked down. "Had it for years."

Megan shook her head, scooping up the blender lid and the seal. "Damn. Too bad."

"What are you doing?" Cecily asked again.

"We dropped your blender parts." Megan located the blade under the edge of the counter and blew off a film of dust.

Anna took a couple of steps toward Cecily, and extended her hand. "Anna Simpson. Sorry to wake you."

"Hi," said Cecily, shaking hands, but looking more asleep than awake. She turned back to Megan. "Why did you drop my blender parts?"

"It was all in pieces. You never washed it. We wanted to make margaritas."

"Without me?"

"You were asleep."

Cecily headed for the kitchen. "So? You know I make them better than you do."

Megan grinned up at Anna. "It's true. She does."

"Did you find them all?" Cecily fixed the plug into the bottom of the sink and turned on the hot water.

"Got 'em." Megan stood up. "We've been out dancing."

Cecily grinned as she squirted some soap into the sink. "With who?"

"Collin and Brett."

"Who's Brett?"

"That other soccer player I told you about. The one I kissed."

"You kissed Brett?" asked Anna, a crease appearing in the center of her forehead.

"It was nothing." Megan waved a dismissive hand.

"What do you mean 'nothing'?"

Megan watched Anna's expression closely. "It was kind of a joke. Why? Do you care?"

"I don't care." The protest came out a little too fast, a little too blasé.

"Anna's got the hots for Brett," Megan said to Cecily, now completely convinced that was the case.

"I do *not*," Anna protested.

"Do so," said Megan.

"He's a bona fide jerk," said Anna.

"But a sexy, bona fide jerk."

Anna paused. "Okay. So he's sexy. But he'd never, not in a million years, make your list."

Cecily set the cleaned parts in the drying rack beside the sink. "They don't have to have *all* the qualities on the list."

"We have to give ourselves a little flexibility," said Megan.

"What's the minimum?" asked Anna.

Megan looked at Cecily, and Cecily quirked an eyebrow back.

"Six," said Megan, making it up on the fly.

"He's got zero," said Anna.

"You want to marry him or sleep with him?" asked Cecily.

"Neither." Anna held up her hands in frustration.

"Just theoretically," said Megan as she reassembled the blender. "If you were to do one or the other?"

"Sleep with him," said Anna. "Definitely. That way he'd leave in the morning."

Cecily sputtered out a laugh, and Megan and Anna joined in.

"Probably leave before the morning," said Cecily.

"You got that right," Anna agreed. "And I'd *never* really do it."

"Never?" asked Megan.

"He's a soccer player."

"So?" Collin was a soccer player. And Megan wasn't ready to say never about him.

"When I say locker-room gossip—" Anna opened the freezer and located a tray of ice cubes "—in this instance, I really mean, *locker-room gossip.*"

"He wouldn't do that." Megan shook her head, still framing the conversation in reference to Collin.

Wait a minute.

What was she saying?

Of course he would.

She blinked and realized both Cecily and Anna were staring at her in frozen silence.

"Forget I said that."

She twisted the glass pitcher into the motor stand.

Anna bent the plastic ice tray to free the cubes, then dumped them into the pitcher with a clatter.

Cecily added the lime, then the tequila, put on the lid and pressed the frappe button. A high-pitched whine filled the kitchen.

When the mixture was blended, Cecily poured it into three glasses.

"You see," said Anna conversationally as they made their way to the living room, "thing is, I need the respect of the Denver Peaks soccer players. It's hard enough getting along in this profession as a woman. If I have a fling with one of them, I'm dead in the water." She took a seat on the carpet, propping her back up against the wood-paneled wall.

Megan and Cecily followed suit.

"She makes a good point," said Cecily.

"I'll say," Megan agreed.

Anna was right to defend herself against gossip.

"Men should never talk to their buddies about their sex lives," said Anna, staring off into space. "Even ten years later. Even if it was only a one-night stand." She focused on Megan and Cecily. "*That* should be on your list."

Cecily straightened. "By God, she's right. It should."

"She's good," said Megan. "Where'd we put the list?"

Cecily jumped up and headed for the computer desk, opening a small drawer.

"I don't know how we missed that."

"Is that *it*?" asked Anna, a lilt of excitement in her voice as Cecily sat back down with the notepad in her hand.

Cecily nodded, rocking the little notepad back and forth. "This is it. The list that started it all."

Anna's eyes lit up, and she scooted across the floor on all fours. "Can I touch it."

Megan laughed. "It's hardly the Shroud of Turin."

Cecily handed the notepad over to Anna. Then she handed her a pen. "Why don't you write that one down?"

Anna took the pen and collapsed back into a sitting position. "You guys should laminate this and sell it on eBay. You'd make a fortune."

Megan smiled, meeting Cecily's laughing eyes.

Anna took a deep breath, pen poised over the paper. "Allow me to say, on this auspicious occasion, that I am both honored and overwhelmed."

"Well, we're embarrassed," said Megan. "I don't know how we let something that important slip by."

Cecily sat back, running a fingertip along the rim of her margarita glass. "So, let's just say you knew he wouldn't brag to his friends…"

Anna looked up from her writing.

"Yeah." Megan settled back for a game of what-if. "If you knew, for sure, he wouldn't brag to his friends…"

"You mean, like he signed in blood or something?" asked Anna.

"Yeah," said Megan. "Let's say he signed in blood."

Anna paused, staring off into space again. She squinted, and one corner of her mouth turned up. Then she pressed her lips together. "Then I'd do him."

Megan and Cecily squealed with laughter.

"And what about Collin?" asked Anna with a knowing smirk, shifting the attention to Megan.

Megan took a sip of her margarita. "He *is* sexy," she admitted.

"He is sexy," Anna agreed.

"But he's conniving," said Megan.

"Conniving?"

Cecily nodded her agreement. "He tried the old wet-puppy routine on Megan."

Anna looked puzzled. "The old wet-puppy routine?"

Megan turned triumphantly to Cecily. "See? I'm not the only one."

"Only one what?" asked Anna. "*What* wet puppy?"

"You know," explained Cecily. "The routine. When a guy pretends to find a wet puppy and brings it home to make a woman think he's got a softer side."

"Guys do that?" asked Anna.

"Collin did that," said Megan.

"Collin has a puppy?" asked Anna.

"Yeah." Megan nodded. "He planted it out in the rain on Lookout Mountain Road so he could rescue it. Poor thing."

Anna stared at the two women. "Collin doesn't have a puppy."

"Sure he does," said Megan. "Little black thing, floppy ears. Very cute. Smells when it's wet."

Anna shook her head. "I was at his house last week. He doesn't have a puppy."

"Well, he's got one now," said Megan.

"He'd never do that."

"I was there. He definitely brought home a puppy."

"I mean, he'd never *plant* a puppy. Not in the rain, not anywhere. Never. Not in a million years. I know that man."

While Anna talked, a hollow feeling formed in the pit of Megan's stomach. "You mean…"

"Hold the phone," said Cecily. "Maybe *she* was in on it."

Anna drew back. *"Me?"* she squeaked. "I didn't even know it happened."

"She looks pretty innocent to me," Megan had to concede.

Cecily's eyes narrowed. "It's still a little too much of a coincidence for my taste."

Anna took a drink of her margarita. "Coincidence or not, I'm telling you, I know this man. If he said he found a puppy, he found a puppy."

"Damn," Megan muttered.

"What?" asked Cecily.

"Sexy *and* compassionate. That means I have to do him and become locker-room gossip."

CHAPTER EIGHT

STANDING in the center rotunda of the Sangre Mall, Collin decided he didn't like the look of the audience. Twenty rows deep in a horseshoe around the broadcast table, they looked edgy, aggressive, ready for trouble.

"Hooligans," Brett mumbled, nodding toward a group of young men in the second row. The short-haired, leather-jacket-clad group must have come early, because five minutes before broadcast it was standing-room only.

"You see any security?" Collin glanced around the mall, seeing nothing but a single uniformed man beside a line of orange surveyor's tape that separated the audience from the broadcast table.

Collin didn't like this. He'd seen plenty of soccer crowds go bad over in Europe, and they rarely found surveyor's tape a huge deterrent.

"Why don't you go sit with Anna?" he asked Brett.

Brett gave him a long, silent look. "That'll guarantee a fight breaks out in the audience."

Collin had been mulling over Megan's theory, deciding it might have merit. "I have a feeling she likes you."

"Yeah, right," Brett scoffed. "You should have heard her last night while we were dancing. I may not be the devil incarnate, but I'm definitely his right-hand man."

"Still," said Collin, "if the crowd gets unruly, it'd be nice if she was there to protect you."

Brett sputtered out a laugh. "Right. Let me just slip into my shining armor. She'll be thrilled to know you care."

One of the technicians came up behind Collin. "We need a sound check."

"Catch you later," said Brett.

"Can you take your seat?" the technician asked Collin.

"Sure."

Collin moved the length of the table, taking his appointed chair next to Megan and putting on his headset. "You sure you want to do this?" he asked her.

She turned to look at him. "Got me okay, Roland?" she said into her microphone.

"Got you. Got Collin," came Roland's voice through the sound system.

"What do you mean, am I sure?" Megan asked Collin. "I've always been sure."

"The crowd looks a little restless."

Megan scanned the sea of people in front of them. "Of course they're restless. Some of them have been waiting for over an hour."

"Some of them look like they're ready for a fight."

She grinned. "That's great."

"Megan—"

"Collin, we're not here to be conciliatory, we're here to be controversial. Remember?"

"It's just—"

"Let 'em shout. Let 'em yell. See those guys over by the food court?"

Collin checked out a cluster of men standing under the taco sign. "Yeah?"

"Those are reporters. If this goes right, we'll make the state news."

"Megan—"

"Thirty seconds," announced Roland.

"I'm worried—"

"Shh," said Megan.

"But—"

"Quiet," said the sound technician.

"Go," came the cue for Cecily.

"Good evening, Denver," sang Cecily. "This is Cecily Cassell coming to you from the Sangre Mall. Welcome to The Perfect Boyfriend show on location with KNOA radio forty-five."

Megan took over. "Tonight's guest is soccer super-star, Collin O'Patrick. As some of you may know, Collin and I had a date last week—"

The crowd roared its approval.

"—Collin didn't get the kiss he wanted, though he did try to sneak one a couple of days later in the Denver Peaks' locker room."

Collin opened his mouth, but Cecily jumped back in. "Tonight we'll talk about that date, how items on The Perfect Boyfriend list might have helped or hindered Collin, and we'll be taking questions from the audience."

"I didn't fail," Collin felt compelled to point out. If

it weren't for the reporter, Megan would have kissed him. She *definitely* would have kissed him.

The masculine side of the audience cheered his assertion.

"I certainly didn't kiss you on the date," said Megan. She turned her attention to the audience. "He wouldn't even buy me a damn hot dog."

The women booed Collin.

Okay. He wasn't sure how to defend himself on that one. He'd refused to buy her refreshments to be ornery, not because he thought it was good dating practice.

"Well, did you put out?" shouted a man from a middle row.

Collin cringed at the crude question.

"Put out for a hot dog?" returned Megan easily. "Ladies, you have a better view of the questioner than I do. Whatever you do, don't date him."

Collin turned to Megan, wondering how she could buy into the guy's quid pro quo stance on sex. "A physical relationship should have nothing to do with the level of expenditure on a date."

"Well, you'd better hope it doesn't," she said, eyes sparkling at his expense.

"A high monetary expenditure shouldn't guarantee sex," he said. "And a low one shouldn't negate it."

"This from a guy who wouldn't even cough up for a lousy hot dog. It goes to the character of the gentleman in question. That would be *you*."

A woman in the back row shouted. "I'll kiss you, Collin."

"That's a very kind offer," said Collin, "but I think you have to stay behind the tape."

Megan smirked.

"First question from the audience," said Cecily, indicating the microphone that had been set up in the aisle.

"Where did you take her?" asked the woman who was standing first in line.

"To a soccer game," said Collin.

The audience groaned.

"I couldn't do dinner and a movie," he defended himself. "It was on the list."

"On a motorcycle in the rain," Megan put in.

That earned Collin another groan.

"I couldn't have been too bad," said Collin. "She kissed me two days later."

Cecily chimed in. "Did she kiss you or did *you* kiss *her*?"

"He started it," accused Megan.

"She finished it." Collin leaned forward and gave the audience a conspiratorial look. "There was definite puckerage."

"I don't believe puckerage is a word," said Cecily.

"Megan can explain it to you later." Collin winked at Cecily.

She grinned at him, shaking her head.

A man stepped up to the microphone next, looking pointedly at Megan. "Do you consider yourself a cock-tease?"

Collin bristled, tensing in his seat.

"I consider myself a discriminating woman who'd

like to date a man who respects and cares for her as a human being, not as a sexual object."

"You're a hard-assed bitch," somebody shouted.

Roland moved from the control booth and positioned himself behind Cecily's chair.

The men in the audience chortled.

Collin felt a subtle shift in the atmosphere. He caught Brett's worried gaze and leaned over to Megan. "Let's shut it down."

"Are you kidding?" she whispered back. "*That's* a sound bite."

"Next question," said Cecily.

A gray-haired woman came up to the microphone, and Collin breathed a sigh of relief.

She waggled her finger at him. "I can't believe that man took you to a sporting event. Shame on you, Collin."

Something about the woman reminded Collin of his grandmother back in Ireland and, despite himself, he felt a twinge of guilt.

"That's all I wanted to say." She squared her shoulders, clutched her black patent purse in front of her, and marched back to her seat.

Next up was one of the young men in leather jackets. Collin tensed up again.

"My old lady read your book," the punk started without preamble. He clutched the microphone stand and his voice rose as he spoke. "You freakin' bitch! You ruined my life!"

That was it.

This was over.

Collin came to his feet, just as the punk hoisted the microphone stand and threw it over the tape barrier. Collin shot out across the table in front of Megan, holding out his hands to protect her from the flying metal stand.

It hit the table with a screech and a clatter. Collin absorbed most of the impact with his forearms, but one of the stand legs caught Cecily in the forehead. Blood instantly welled up at her hairline.

Before Collin could choose between Megan and Cecily, Roland hoisted Cecily in his arms and headed into the women's clothing store behind them.

Some of the crowd had come to their feet. Some were yelling, and a few arguments broke out between the spectators. Still others were craning their necks for a look. The security guard had grabbed the punk, and a couple of other men were helping hold him still.

The worst seemed to be over, but Collin wasn't taking any chances. He dropped the microphone stand to the floor, wrapped one arm around Megan and lifted her from her chair, following the path that Roland had taken.

"Cecily," Megan breathed in a worried voice.

Collin didn't have to rush her away from the crowd. She was practically running after her friend.

"Did it look bad?" she asked Collin. "Was she bleeding?"

"She was bleeding a little," said Collin.

Megan swore.

One of the sales clerks motioned them toward a back exit, and before Collin knew it he was outside in the lighted parking lot of the mall.

Megan broke free of Collin and rushed for Cecily.

"Did you call an ambulance?" Collin asked Roland.

"On its way," said Roland. "I think she's going to be fine."

Collin resisted an urge to ream the man out over the lack of security. Roland knew the women's show was controversial. He should have expected the crowd could get unruly.

A helicopter sounded overhead, its lights appearing from beyond the roof of the mall.

"You called in a chopper?" Collin asked as the searchlight hit them. Of course, he wanted Cecily to get immediate medical attention, but the cut hadn't honestly looked all that bad.

"It's a news crew," said Roland.

"News?" Megan perked up, shading her eyes.

"This is good, right?" asked Cecily.

"It's only good if you're okay," said Megan, rubbing Cecily's arm.

"I'm fine," said Cecily. "Should I let them see the blood?"

"Will you people stop?" Collin shouted. "This isn't Jerry Springer."

All three heads turned toward him and stared in silence. The ambulance siren sounded in the distance, bouncing off the high stone walls of the mall.

Megan spoke. "It's not like we cut her on purpose for the ratings. But…" She gestured to Cecily "…this is news."

"A man did go berserk during our broadcast," said Cecily.

"Can't buy publicity like that," Roland agreed.

The ambulance rounded the corner of the building, red lights flashing, sirens blocking further conversation.

As soon as it came to a stop the medics jumped out and assessed Cecily. When they helped her into the back of the vehicle, Megan climbed in with her.

"You're going to get those two killed," said Collin in disgust as the ambulance pulled away. Its lights were still flashing, but they'd killed the siren.

"No more remote broadcasts," said Roland.

"You think that solves the problem?"

"Of course."

Collin opened his mouth to argue, but then he remembered that he was done. This was his last broadcast for KNOA. From now on, Megan, Cecily and Roland could do whatever the hell they wanted with the radio show.

He was going back to soccer. Straight up, no frills, no paparazzi soccer.

Megan stared hard at the front page of the evening paper—the second one in a week featuring her and Collin. Although this time it featured a lot more of Collin than her.

Because he'd thrown himself in front of her.

Because he'd used his body to save her.

Because, apparently, he wasn't as much of a jerk as he'd made himself out to be.

She kicked off her sandals and slid down in the wooden chair at her tiny kitchen table, flattening the newspaper.

"Soccer Star Collin O'Patrick Saves Radio Host" said the caption. "Story on page two."

Megan didn't need to turn to page two to know she owed Collin her thanks. Her gaze wandered to the telephone on the little round table at the end of her sofa. She was definitely going to thank him.

Only decision was where, when and how.

The telephone would be fast, but impersonal.

Stopping by would be more polite.

Maybe she should drop off a card?

Flowers? Nah, he seemed way too masculine for flowers.

Chocolate? Did athletes eat junk food?

Maybe she should go with a fruit basket? After all he'd done, practically risking his life, the least she could do was cough up for a gift.

She stood up, smoothing the front of her sleeveless, lightweight denim dress. Fruit basket it was. Megan stepped into her sandals and scooped up the car keys.

Then she hesitated at the door. Was there a latent homosexual message in a fruit basket?

She shook her head. Forget it. She was overanalyzing this whole thing. She'd drop down to Merlin's on the corner, pick up a fruit basket, drive over to Collin's, and show him she had dignity and class.

Right.

She headed out.

Luckily, Merlin's had a great selection. She browsed her way through the store, gradually talking herself into larger baskets. In the end, she chose one with a pineapple, a bunch of bananas, round things in every color of the rainbow, red and green grapes, and some kind of foliage cascading down from the wicker handle, obscuring a fancy purple bow.

Feeling satisfied with the quality of her gift, Megan settled it in the back of her car and pulled out into the evening traffic. If this baby didn't say thank you, nothing did.

It took her about twenty minutes to get to Collin's.

It was a struggle to hold onto the basket and ring the bell at the same time, but she managed, and then settled the basket in front of her—partly to make a good impression and partly because she couldn't hold the darn thing any other way.

His door opened.

"Hello?" Collin peered around the greenery. "Who's there?"

"It's Megan."

"Megan?" He moved the pineapple to one side, brows slanting together. "Oh. There you are. Did you rob a fruit stand?"

Okay, now she felt gauche instead of classy, and her arms were starting to ache. "I came to say thank you."

"Thank you?"

"You know. For yesterday."

He didn't say anything.

"For saving me."

A grin grew on his face. "From the rogue microphone stand?"

Now he was laughing at her. Obviously one heroic

act did not change a sow's ear into a silk purse. Her first impression was right. He was a jerk, not a gentleman.

She sighed. "Yeah. You think you could maybe take this thing out of my arms?"

"Sure." He hoisted it away. "Good God, it weighs a *ton*."

"I just wanted to…" Her voice trailed away.

He paused, gazing down at her, the mocking expression leaving his face. "And it was very nice of you. Come in." He nodded his head to the side, indicating the open door.

"No, that's okay."

"Come in, Megan. I sure as hell can't eat all of this myself."

Megan bit down on a self-conscious grin. She hadn't stopped to think that he lived alone. Maybe he could be the snack man at the Panthers' next game.

As soon as she crossed the threshold she heard the puppy whining in the kitchen. His little nose was pressed up against a plastic child gate as he struggled to get out.

Collin pushed the door shut and set the enormous fruit basket down on the coffee table. "You mind if I let him out? He gets upset when he's not with me."

"Of course not."

Collin opened the gate and the puppy nearly wagged his body in half, wiggling his way around Collin's legs. He scooted across the hardwood floor, coming to a skidding stop at Megan's feet, circling her twice, then heading back to Collin.

"How's Cecily?" asked Collin.

"She's fine. Roland can't dote on her enough."

"He's afraid she'll sue. And she should."

"She's not suing anybody."

Collin gestured to his couch. "They should have had more security."

Megan sat down on the big, leather sofa. "These things happen. The guy was a wing-nut. I don't know why you'd ever align yourself with somebody like that."

Collin sat down in an armchair while the puppy scampered across the floor to chew on a bright orange ball. "I never aligned myself with that guy."

"Well, he sure as hell wasn't on my side."

"Just because I don't believe in using cheap tricks to attract women, doesn't mean I advocate treating them like dirt. The guy was an asshole. His girlfriend was lucky to read your book."

Megan sat up straight, leaning slightly forward. "*What* was that you just said?"

"Don't get all excited. I'm glad she read your book because it made her turf that guy, not because I agree with your manipulative techniques."

"Candy and flowers are a time-honored tradition."

"You recommend expensive jewelry."

Megan grinned self-consciously. "Diamonds show a certain…commitment to the relationship, don't you think?"

"Forgive me if I prefer honesty to bribery."

"I never said I had anything against honesty."

He leaned forward in his chair, bringing his face to within a foot of hers. "You want to know what I think?"

Her smile grew as she focused on his intense eyes. "I'm dying to know what you think."

He took a breath. "I think a real relationship has to be based on honesty. It's not about who gets sex and who gets jewelry. It's about getting past the façade and getting to know each other as real people."

"A man who loves me in sweatpants," Megan muttered under her breath.

"What was that?"

Megan cleared her throat. "It's from the list. 'Next man I date is going to love me in sweatpants.'"

Collin tilted his head and gave her a cocky grin. "Well, let's not get *too* carried away."

She socked him in the arm.

He caught her hand and held it against his biceps. His gaze went unexpectedly soft. "There are a million guys out there who would love you in sweatpants."

A warm glow worked its way from her fingertips to her chest.

He slid the pad of his thumb across her palm, and a jolt of electricity jump-started her system. She quickly drew her hand away, rubbing it against the side of her dress.

Megan cleared her throat again, glancing around the room to distract herself from the sexy gray eyes that suddenly seemed to know too much about her. "So, uh, why did you keep the puppy?"

Collin turned to where the ungainly pup was scampering across the floor in pursuit of the ball. "Rocky?"

"Is that what you named him?"

Collin shrugged. "I figured we found him in the mountains."

Megan couldn't help but smile. "It's cute."

"Thank you."

But it didn't answer her question. "So, why did you keep him?"

"He was a little, wet puppy on the side of the highway. Who wouldn't have kept him?"

"Lots of people wouldn't have kept him."

"You're cynical."

"I'm not cynical. I'm realistic. You brought him home. You bought him a ball. I'm guessing you didn't have that kiddy gate when he arrived."

Collin gave another shrug.

"If I check the kitchen, am I going to find a soft, cozy doggy bed?"

He slanted her a look of disdain.

She started to rise.

"Okay. Okay." He stopped her. "So I once knew a pup like him."

Something in his tone hit her square in the chest, and she sat back down. "What do you mean, a pup like him?"

"When I was a little boy."

"You mean black?"

Collin set his jaw, a faraway look coming into his eyes, along with the barest flicker of pain.

"You don't have to tell me." She quickly backed off.

He shook his head. "It's okay. When I was eight years old, back in Killarney, my neighbor's dad dumped a litter of pups at the side of the road." Collin's accent thickened. "I guess he thought somebody would come along and pick them up."

He stood up, retrieved the rubber ball and gently tossed it down the hallway. Rocky streaked after it, his big back feet slipping on the floor.

Megan was almost afraid to ask. "Did they?"

"When my neighbor told me what his dad had done, I rode my bike five miles down the valley to rescue them."

Megan's chest tightened. "You brought them home?"

"Three of them. My dad thrashed my butt for being so stupid."

Rocky toddled back with the ball in his mouth.

"He *what*?"

Collin shook his head and let out a chopped laugh. "Wasn't the first time. Sure wasn't the last time. I was an energetic and adventurous young lad."

Megan stood up. She didn't know what to say.

Collin turned at the sound of her movement as he threw the ball again. He stopped and took in her expression, voice going softer. "Hey, it wasn't as bad as it sounds. We were Catholic. Spare the rod and spoil the child."

"It's horrible," she said.

"It wasn't the thrashing that upset me."

"No?"

"No."

"Then what was it?"

The faraway look came back again. "It was the fourth puppy."

"There was a fourth puppy?"

Collin nodded as he crouched down to take the ball from Rocky.

She wanted to reach out and touch him, somehow comfort him. "What happened to it?"

"Never did find out. I hope somebody picked him up. He wasn't around when I got there. I called and called, but there was just the other three."

Megan felt tears well up in her eyes, and she reached out to lightly touch his shoulder.

He turned, and she sniffed.

"Hey." He straightened, wrapping an arm around her and giving her a squeeze. "It was a long time ago. After my dad got over being mad, he let me keep the dogs. I worked my butt off paying for food for the next ten years, but they all had long and happy lives."

Megan's chest tightened. Sexy *and* compassionate. Hoo boy. "You're not making this up, are you?" she asked him.

"Making this up?"

She tipped her head to look up at him. "You know, to make me get all soft and mushy so I'll want to kiss you."

Collin wiped the single tear that had leaked out the corner of her eye. "You wanna kiss me?"

"Is that a no?"

He grinned. "I'm the honesty guy, remember?"

"That's not an answer."

"You are one cynical woman."

She waited.

"Of *course* it's a no," he finally said, gray eyes twinkling. "I'm not making any of it up."

She gave in and smiled back, her heart thudding with anticipation. "Okay," she admitted. "Then, yeah, I wanna kiss you."

"Good." He shifted his body toward her, turning to press his taut frame against hers. His voice dropped to a husky rumble next to her ear. "Cause, I sure wanna kiss you."

Her nerve endings pulsed. Okay. This was it. Not a lot of room to turn back now.

"You ready?" he asked.

She shook her head. Then she nodded.

He tipped his head toward her.

She whispered on a sigh. "The least you could do is make me a blender drink so I can keep my dignity."

He chuckled low and sexy, his lips rapidly closing in on hers. "Hate to be the one to tell you this, darlin'. But your dignity is toast."

CHAPTER NINE

THE instant Collin's lips touched Megan's, his laughter evaporated. Desire hijacked his brain, and a cascade of sensation roared in his ears as the world paused for breath.

Rocky's toenails no longer scratched the floor. The kids on the sidewalk no longer shouted. And the clock in the corner no longer ticked off the seconds of the evening.

Nothing existed but Megan. The satin of her skin, the rose scent of her shampoo, the sweet mint taste of her soft lips.

They parted.

In a split second, he was answering her invitation. He deepened the kiss, tightening one arm around her waist while his other hand moved up to possessively cup her face.

He stroked the pad of his thumb down her jaw line, along her smooth neck and through to the back of her neck, drawing her closer still.

In answer, her arms twined around his waist, small hands pressing into his spine, twisting fistfuls of his T-shirt as a moan escaped her lips.

He whispered her name.

She molded against him.

He arched her back, kissing her, deeply, thoroughly, endlessly.

When he was sure he wouldn't last another second without ripping his way into her little dress, Collin broke the kiss. He held her tight, tucking her head against his shoulder, stroking her hair as he struggled to bring his breathing under control. Somehow he had to remember he was a man of principles.

"We have to stop," he rasped, talking to himself as much as to her, yet still reveling in the lingering scent of roses.

"We do?" she responded, her soft, hot breath puffing through the cotton of his T-shirt to warm the skin of his shoulder.

Of *course* they had to stop. Surely she realized they were in deep trouble here. He nodded against her. "This is nuts."

She touched her hands to his shoulders, pulling back her flushed face to grin unrepentantly. "At the risk of disagreeing with you…"

An answering smile tugged at the corners of his mouth. The children were shouting outside again. The clock was ticking. He was going to make it.

"There's no reason to stop," she surprised him by saying, moving her thinly clad body against his.

"Megan." His voice was low, with an edge of warning. He knew she liked playing with fire, but surely even *she* knew they couldn't keep this up for more than thirty seconds without consequences.

"We're consenting adults," she said, eyes closing as she came up on tiptoe and parted her swollen lips.

His heart rate sky-rocketed, and his hands went to her bare shoulders, pushing her firmly back down on her heels. "You don't mean that."

"Well, we *are*," she pouted.

"I mean you don't mean that the way it sounded."

She paused, eyebrows going up, jewel eyes shimmering expectantly. "How—exactly—did it sound?"

He stared at her, hard. "Like you want to go to bed with me."

She didn't deny the blunt statement, didn't slap him. In fact, she didn't react at all. She just stared unblinkingly up at him and let him draw his own conclusions.

And he was drawing conclusions.

He was drawing conclusions that she didn't even want to know about.

"Collin," she chided. "For a man with the reflexes of a jungle cat, you're sure a little slow on the uptake."

He raked a hand through his hair. "We've been fighting since the minute we met."

"Turns out it *was* foreplay."

He paused, taking in her tousled blonde hair, her dark lips, her spectacular green eyes, the thick lashes that raised his blood pressure with every blink. His gaze dipped to the blue dress that hugged her mouth-watering curves. Then it moved down toned thighs and shapely tanned calves. Even her feet were beautiful.

What the hell was he doing?

Here was a gorgeous, sexy, savvy woman all but handing him a no-strings fling on a silver platter, and he was *arguing* with her?

His hands relaxed on her bare shoulders, no longer holding her away. Instead, he pushed her hair back from her forehead, enjoying the smoothness of her skin, the texture and bounce of her curls.

She wanted to go for it? Okay by him.

He gazed into her emerald eyes and gave her a long, slow grin. "You call *that* foreplay?" He shook his head and clicked his tongue. "Baby, let me show you foreplay."

She tipped her head to a challenging angle. "Bring it on, O'Patrick."

"Until you scream for mercy."

"Scream? Don't you think you might be setting the bar a little high?"

"I'm a classic overachiever." With a hand on the small of her back, he drew her into the cradle of his thighs. "First thing we do is forget all about those famous, lightning-fast reflexes."

He moved his hand to cradle her head with one palm, kissing her hairline, her temple, her cheek, even the tip of her straight nose. "You got anywhere you have to be?"

Her hands slipped down and tightened on his biceps. "Not tonight, I don't."

"Good." He bent down and scooped her off the floor in an easy motion.

She tensed for a second, but then relaxed against his chest. "We going somewhere?"

"My bedroom."

"So fast?"

He chuckled. "Trust me on this one."

He carried her down the hall, then through his bedroom and onto his private deck. There he set her on her feet next to the hot tub. The sun was just slipping behind the Rockies, and the cool evening breeze rustled the oak trees and juniper bushes.

He reached around her back and rested his fingertips on the zipper of her dress. "Seems to me we had a deal about a kiss in your underwear."

He took her smile as permission and slipped the zipper slowly down her back, watching her eyes to make sure she was with him on this.

When the zipper stopped at her waist, she shrugged her shoulders. The cotton dress slipped down to pool at her feet. "Deal's a deal," she said.

Collin took a step back to drink in her beauty. "I think I got the good end of this deal."

He reached for her waist with both hands, wrapping them above the wispy, high-cut panties. The contrast in texture and color between her skin and his turned him on. He strummed his thumb over her flat, smooth abdomen.

She inhaled sharply. "As I recall, you weren't exactly a slouch in yours."

He took a long, leisurely look at her body. "You're wearing cream satin and lace. I was wearing sweaty black Jockeys."

She took a step forward, tugging his T-shirt from the waistband of his jeans. "But everything else was bare."

He grunted. "That was good?"

"*That* was very good. It was all I could do to string together a coherent sentence."

"Well, you're pretty good under fire."

She pulled his shirt off over his head. "So are you."

They both drank in each other's bodies for a silent moment. Though he wanted nothing more than to scoop her up again and carry her straight back to his bed, Collin was determined not to rush this.

"You want a glass of wine?"

She hesitated, gaze flicking to the button on his fly. Then she looked back up at his face. "Sure."

He sucked in a desperate breath. Man, oh, man, this was going to be tough. "Meet you in the hot tub?"

She reached for the back of her bra. "You got it."

He abruptly turned back to the house. If he saw her bare breasts, he was done for.

Rocky was sound asleep in the middle of the hallway. He didn't even stir as Collin located a bottle of Merlot and a pair of glasses.

Collin made his way slowly back down the hallway, taking deep breaths and giving himself a pep talk as he walked. He prayed she'd be concealed by the bubbles when he got back. If she was naked, he was dead.

His prayers were answered.

The foaming water covered her to her bare shoulders. The sunset had disappeared, and the first stars were winking in the blue-black sky.

She stretched her arms across the edge of the hot tub, watching him light a few candles and pop the cork on the wine bottle.

"Merlot okay?" he asked as he poured the first glass.

"Sounds wonderful," she answered, her sultry voice all but hanging in the night air.

He took another deep breath and handed her the glass. Her damp fingertips, hot from the water, tingled against his own. Collin quickly drew away and set the other wineglass on the wide, cedar lip of the tub.

She raised her eyebrows in the direction of his jeans.

Though stripping in front of her was a level of eroticism that might be the death of him, fair was fair.

Without looking at her, he quickly shucked his pants and climbed in.

"Land speed record or what?" she muttered as he settled across the tub from her, hoping to give himself a few minutes to get under control.

"Didn't want to tempt you unfairly," he responded, reaching for his wineglass.

She sidled along the bench seat toward him. "I'll try to control myself."

He braced himself as she drew nearer.

She sat there for a moment. Then she bumped a wet shoulder up against his biceps. "Uh, Collin."

"Yeah?"

"I'm no expert." He could hear the smile in her voice. "I mean, not like you. But doesn't making me scream from foreplay involve a little…touching?"

Suddenly, he was tired of the pretense. He'd never

been much good at games of one-upmanship. In fact, he disdained people who used them. Instead of answering, he stretched his arm along the edge of the hot tub, wrapping it around Megan's slippery, wet body, drawing her close, sliding her across his thighs until she was cradled in his lap.

"I'm afraid I did," he said frankly, letting his hands roam her bare back, his body growing taut with desire as he watched the foaming water swirl around her breasts.

"Did what?" Her voice was slightly breathless. She put one hand on his shoulder to steady herself.

"Set the bar too high."

Megan quirked an eyebrow.

"Truth is, I'm shaking with the need to make love with you."

Her mocking smile disappeared, and her wet arms twined around his neck, bringing her soft breasts up against his chest. "I'm adding that to the list," she whispered.

"The list?"

She moved her lips closer to his. "Yeah. The next man I date will be shaking with the need to make love with me."

Collin completed the kiss, giving in to the countless sensations of Megan. Within seconds the world disappeared once again. Dimly, he realized that they had to get out of the hot tub and back inside to his bed

But his lips were too busy kissing her. His skin was too hot from her touch. And his hands were too happy exploring her breasts for a coherent thought to make it out of his brain.

She turned in his lap, straddling him. Her breasts were out of the water, and he fixated on her coral nipples. Unable to stop himself, he bent his head and took one into his mouth—laving it, tonguing it, and drawing it erect.

Megan moaned his name. Her mouth opened against the top of his head, and her fingertips tangled in his short hair.

He clasped her bottom, pulling her closer, lips caressing her breasts, fingers exploring the length of her thighs.

Her hands skimmed down his chest, over his stomach, between their bodies until she gripped him with her velvet palm.

Her name was a guttural exclamation torn from deep inside him. He captured her face, and drew her down for a frantic, passionate kiss—mouths open, tongues seeking.

She moved her hand, and fireworks began percolating at the base of his brain. Dimly, he realized this was way too fast. They hadn't even left the damn hot tub. But then he was lifting her, positioning her, and she was guiding him inside.

The heat of her body enveloped him, and Collin lost what little was left of his reasoning power.

He kissed her, strained against her. His hands roamed her skin even as hers dug into the muscles of his back. He wanted to explain, wanted to apologize, but the only word he formed was her name, over and over again.

Trying to hold himself back was useless. His body was a steaming train running faster and harder and more wildly out of control.

She whispered his name, kissed the edge of his ear.

Her teeth bit down gently, and her sweet, rhythmic breath fanned against him. She kissed his temple, his hairline, his cheek. Then her mouth found his again and her hands slipped down to his buttocks.

She tightened her grip, pressing him against her.

He came up off the seat, carrying her with him, holding her tighter, straining to get closer, closer.

Her arms went around his neck, and her kisses turned staccato, her tongue keeping with the beat of his runaway body.

He closed his eyes, and the fireworks in his brain turned to rockets, bursting in a blaze of sound and fury and fire. He all but shouted her name.

As aftershocks pulsed through his body, he slowly sat back down on the bench.

"You okay?" he breathed, as soon as it was possible to form words.

"Yeah," she breathed back. "I didn't scream. But I gotta tell you, O'Patrick, it was damn close."

He felt a weak chuckle ripple through his body. If he had the strength, he'd actually laugh.

She pulled back, cupping his face in her hands and staring into his eyes.

"Holy cow," she said. "I mean, *holy cow*." She planted a final, soft, lingering kiss on his lips. "You are one serious overachiever."

A wave of pure satisfaction washed through Collin. "And here I thought it was too fast."

"I prefer to think of it as efficient."

Wait a minute.

He paused.

And frowned.

He didn't like the sound of that. "Efficient?"

Megan shook her head. "You hit a grand slam, Collin. Quit looking for more compliments."

"A grand slam?"

"Big time."

He kissed her. Then he kissed her again. Then again. Damned if he wasn't willing to start over.

But he pulled back. "Allow me to say that, as a soccer player, you make a fantastic lover."

She grinned and his chest tightened. "Fantastic?"

He nodded. "Fantastic."

Her eyes turned to soft jade, and they stared at each other in silence. The candles flickered in the nighttime breeze and the stars blossomed to full strength above them. If ever there was a moment to stop time, this was it.

Finally, he reached out to brush a lock of hair from her cheek. "You hungry?"

She sighed. "A little."

"Want a pineapple?"

Collin was rewarded with a self-conscious grin.

"Can I buy you dinner?" he asked.

"A corn dog?"

"Seafood at Maddigo's. Or I could order in." A vision of Megan eating pizza on his couch, her hair dripping wet, wrapped in his big white robe, bloomed enticingly in his mind. He didn't want to disturb their chemistry, didn't want to share her with the world just yet.

"I'm easy," she said.

He cocked his head. "Easy? I don't think so."

She socked him in the shoulder.

He caught her hand, and stared deep into her eyes. "But you are definitely worth the trouble. You like pizza?"

Megan's body was still humming at the close of business the next day. Jennifer and the rest of the staff had left at four-thirty, but Megan still held out hope that she might hear from Victor McKnight of Ferretti Industries about her ideas for commercials with Anna's soccer team. As the clock ticked down to five, she realized it would be at least another day, probably even next week before she got a response.

She sighed and picked up her keyring, slinging her purse over her shoulder, getting ready to head upstairs and see if something had magically appeared in her refrigerator. Or, better still, to see if Collin might have left a message on her home machine. Not that he didn't know her work number. Not that he couldn't have stopped by if he'd felt like seeing her again.

She gave another sigh, a bigger one this time. How had she suddenly become this woman who waited by the telephone?

As she stood up her door burst open.

It was Anna.

She rushed in, slamming the door shut behind her, pressing her back and hands tight against it as if she were keeping somebody out.

"Anna?" Megan walked around the desk.

"You have to come with me," Anna blurted out.

"With you where?"

"To the game."

"What game? When game?"

"The Denver Peaks game. Now. Tonight. Brett just phoned and invited me."

After the first sentence, Anna's words stopped penetrating.

Collin had a game tonight? No wonder he hadn't called. Megan told herself it was pathetic to feel such a sense of relief, but she couldn't help the small smile that crept out.

"This isn't funny," shrieked Anna.

"What's not funny?" asked Megan.

"The game."

"Okay…"

Anna's eyes went a little wild. "*Brett* asked me to the game."

"But that's a good thing," said Megan. "I still think you two would make—"

"It's a terrible thing." Anna stepped further into the room, whisking her long hair behind her ear. "I don't know what he means by it. Is it a setup? Is it a trap? Is it, like, a real date?"

"Why would it be a trap?"

Guilt flashed across Anna's face.

"Anna?"

"Fine. It might be a trap, because I slept with him."

"You *what*?" Now that was a stunning revelation.

Anna began pacing distractedly. "After the remote broadcast. He was just so sweet and protective when the crowd got rowdy.

"And then again last night. Because he was still there. Okay, so technically, I'm not sure we actually stopped sleeping together in between. We did get up and eat and everything, but..." She paused in her pacing. "Please come with me."

"Of course I'll come with you. But are you sure you want me there?"

"Yes! If it's locker-room gossip he's planning, you have to save me."

"He's not planning locker-room gossip."

"You don't know Brett."

A smile twitched on Megan's face. "Not as well as you do, apparently."

"Don't mock me."

"Hey, if it makes you feel any better, I slept with Collin—"

"You *did*?"

"—so if there's locker-room gossip, we're going down together."

Anna waved her hands. "Back up. Back up. You slept with Collin?"

Megan headed for the door. "I did."

"Was he good?"

"Was *Brett* good?"

Anna flushed. "God, yes."

Megan chuckled and shook her head. "I guess soccer's not the only thing those boys excel at."

Anna smiled, and her shoulders seemed to relax. "So, you'll come to the game?"

Megan opened the door. "Sure. What's the worst that can happen?"

"Locker-room gossip and a news crew."

"I wish your imagination wasn't quite so vivid."

As they neared the end of the second half, with no sign of a news crew, Anna finally stopped fidgeting.

"You think maybe he just wants to see me again?" she asked Megan.

"There is definitely that possibility," said Megan, her attention distracted by Collin, who was making a run down the field.

Two defenders came up to meet him. He outmaneuvered one of them, but the other forced him to pass. Another Peaks team member got the ball, and they were still making good progress down the field.

"It makes me nervous," Anna stated.

"What makes you nervous?"

Collin got clear at the edge of the goal crease, calling for the ball. His teammate passed it, but the pass went too far ahead. The goalie had come out and was racing to beat him.

"Brett wanting to see me again," said Anna.

"As nervous as being the subject of locker-room gossip?"

Collin suddenly turned on a sprint. Wow. He tapped the ball sideways, out of the path of the rushing goalie, then he caught it with the inside of his left foot and sent it soaring into the goal.

The crowd roared, coming to its feet.

Megan and Anna stood with them.

"No. Not as nervous as being locker-room gossip." Anna swallowed. "I guess."

The score was three to two for the Peaks, with only three minutes left on the clock.

"Maybe he likes you," said Megan as they took their seats again.

"After all this time?"

"Maybe he's liked you all this time."

Anna frowned. "He has a funny way of showing it."

"You like him?" asked Megan.

Anna glanced down. "Yeah. Kinda. He surprised me."

"Then maybe you should give him a chance."

She sighed, then smiled and tucked her hair behind her ears. "What about you? You like Collin?"

A warm glow worked its way through Megan's system as she remembered lying in his big bed last night, talking for hours. Her voice went soft. "Yeah. Kinda. He surprised me, too."

Anna hopped to her feet. "Then let's go meet them at the locker room."

"Wait a minute. I wasn't invited to the locker room." And last time Megan had gone into that room, things hadn't turned out so well. Besides, she had no idea if Collin wanted to see her again. Better to let him call than to ambush him.

Anna linked her arm through Megan's, pulling her to her feet. "We'll wait in the hall. We're in this together."

"But—"

"No buts." Anna started walking, and Megan

scrambled to keep from being jerked into another spectator's lap.

"Collin's not expecting me," said Megan as they headed down the concrete stairs.

"So what? You're with me. The fact that he might be around too is merely a coincidence."

"Anna, he's on the team."

"Just act casual."

"You're such a big talker when I'm the one who might be embarrassed."

Anna laughed. "Funny how that works, isn't it?"

At the bottom of the stairs, they came to a security guard at the door to the locker-room tunnel. Anna gave the man her name, and he opened the steel door for them. Several kids in the audience cast envious looks in their direction.

Megan thought about offering to trade places.

As the door clicked shut behind them three shrill whistle blasts signaled the end of the game. The home crowd cheered the Peaks' victory, and dozens of people leaned over the rail above the tunnel to watch the players exit.

Megan took a deep breath, anxious to spot Collin, yet dreading spotting Collin. Last night had been fantastic—not just the sex, though that had been nothing short of amazing. But Collin had let his guard down, and she'd let her guard down, and it felt as though they'd connected on a whole new level.

But that was last night. He might be less than thrilled at having her show up in the cold light of day. Or maybe

Anna was right, and Megan had become locker-room gossip. She shuddered, taking a subconscious step backward as the team members poured in from the field.

Marc Allendale was the first to appear. Anna had introduced Megan to him at the practice on Sunday.

"Hey, Megan," he greeted, then turned his attention to Anna, slowing to a stop in front of her.

His voice went lower. "Hi, Anna."

"Hi, Marc."

"How're you doing?"

"Fine, thanks. Nice game."

He inched a little closer. "Thanks."

Suddenly Brett appeared next to Anna. His arm went around her waist and he gave her a quick kiss on the temple.

Then he shot a glare at Marc. "Back off, Allendale."

Marc held up his palms. "Hey, just talkin' to her."

Brett's eyebrows went up. "Stop."

Megan smiled to herself. This was definitely not the behavior of a man interested in disparaging Anna's reputation with his teammates.

Marc glanced from Anna's slightly flushed face back to Brett again. "So that's the way it is?"

"That's the way it is," Brett confirmed with a sharp nod.

Marc nodded and backed away.

"Megan." Collin's voice sounded close to her ear.

Her stomach cramped.

"What are you doing here?"

It cramped tighter.

"She came with me," Anna quickly put in.

"Great," said Collin. He twined his fingers through Megan's and gave her hand a squeeze.

Her stomach relaxed a little, and she dared to look up at him.

He smiled openly, then glanced at Brett and Anna. "So, we all going somewhere to eat?"

"Sounds good," said Brett. He lowered his voice and spoke to Anna. "You mind waiting around while we shower?"

"I'd rather wait than be seen in public with you looking like that."

Brett grinned at her. "Smart woman."

Collin cocked his head at Megan. "You mind?"

"I don't mind."

They gazed into each other's eyes for a long moment.

"Missed you," Collin mouthed, and Megan's chest tightened. She instantly relived all the passion and laughter from last night.

"Me, too," she whispered.

Collin squeezed her hand again. "Don't you go anywhere."

CHAPTER TEN

"So what's with you and Anna?" Collin asked Brett, buttoning up his shirt while he slipped into his running shoes.

He'd seen the way his teammate had looked at Anna in the hallway. Seemed like Megan was right. Something was definitely going on between them.

Brett tossed his cleats into the bottom of his locker. "Since I practically saved her life at the remote broadcast, she took me out for dinner. Least she could do."

"Oh, yeah, that gray-haired woman with the black leather purse was about to go postal."

"Hey, there was a fracas. I got her out."

"A *fracas*?"

"Yeah."

Collin bit back a laugh. "You sure it wasn't a skirmish or a tussle?"

"Back off."

"So you turned this imaginary white knight thing into a free dinner."

"I paid."

"After she offered?"

"Yeah." Brett crossed his arms over his chest. "So?"

That didn't sound like Brett.

Collin grinned. "It's really too bad you don't like her much."

"It was just dinner."

"So what's tonight?"

"Just dinner again."

"But you don't actually like her?"

Brett shrugged and turned to latch his locker. "She's okay. But let's talk about *you* and the iron maiden of The Perfect Boyfriend show."

Collin tensed.

Brett turned to check out his expression and chuckled. "Getting ready to defend the lady's honor?"

"She's not as tough as she pretends to be," said Collin.

"*I* never thought she was." Brett laughed. "You ready?"

"Yeah." They headed for the locker-room door. "You won't…"

"Won't what?" asked Brett.

"Nothing."

Brett's face broke into a wide grin. "You going to start using the list?"

"Never."

"We could pick up some flowers on the way. You know, give her a *little surprise*."

"I don't do little surprises. Or make blender drinks. And I couldn't do an Australian accent to save my life."

"But you do open doors. And you always pay. And on your first date, you came home with a slobbery dog."

"Rocky's not slobbery."

Brett reached for the door handle. "You've been doomed from minute one."

"Give me one minute," Megan said to her receptionist over the phone. "Then send him in."

She quickly pulled a mirror out of her desk drawer, made sure her hair was neat and nothing was stuck between her teeth. Then she straightened the items on the top of her desk and took a quick glance at the credenza behind her.

Nobody from Ferretti Industries had *ever* stopped by her office, never mind Victor McKnight himself. Her stomach fluttered. They must really like her ideas with Anna and the Panthers.

Ten seconds left.

Megan sat back down, took a deep breath, and folded her hands on the desk.

The door opened, and Jennifer ushered the forty-ish, tall and slightly graying Victor McKnight in through the door.

Megan rose, rounded the desk and extended her hand. "Mr. McKnight."

He shook. "Victor, please."

"Victor, then. Thank you, Jennifer." She gestured to her meeting table. "Please sit down."

Jennifer closed the office door behind her, and Megan took a seat across from Victor.

"I'll get right to the point, Megan," he said.

Megan nodded, picking up a pen and turning a pad of paper toward her. "All right."

"We have a mild interest in your ideas for Anna Simpson and the Panthers soccer team."

Mild? Megan forced herself to keep a poker face. She'd been hoping for a lot more than just mild.

"However, we are willing to take the campaign and run with it."

Okay, this was getting better.

Victor cleared his throat. "On one condition."

"A condition?" Megan's brain scrambled to figure out what condition they might put on Anna and the team. No rival sponsorship? A favorable endorsement rate if Anna's Olympic team won gold…

"We'd like to make it a package deal," said Victor.

Megan put down the pen and sat back in her chair. "What kind of package?" Did they want the entire Olympic team?

Victor's fingertips drummed on the table. He looked nervous. What? Did he want to *date* Anna or something?

"We'd like Collin O'Patrick to endorse some of our athletic products."

A stone dropped through the middle of Megan's stomach. Keeping a poker face wasn't even an option.

"We read the papers, Megan. We know you've been spending time with him."

"But…" Her voice was little more than a squeak.

"A date? Then a second radio show?"

Megan shook her head, accessing enough of her brain cells to participate in the conversation. "Collin won't do ads."

"Ask him," said Victor.

"He's adamant," she responded.

"Give it a shot."

"He's resolute."

"Remember, we pay you for creativity."

Megan took a deep breath. "He's almost evangelical."

Victor stood up, dropping his business card on the table. "That's my private cell number. Give it some thought. You get us Collin O'Patrick, and we'll make sure every home in America knows Anna Simpson's face."

With a businesslike nod, he turned and left the room.

As the door closed behind him Megan went limp.

Get Collin to endorse athletic wear? He'd probably prefer to hang by his thumbs in hot oil. Or face a herd of stampeding buffalo. Or jump out of a speeding train. Off a trestle bridge. Into a gorge.

Jennifer slipped in through the office door. "Well?" she asked, expression expectant.

Megan slid Victor's card a couple inches to the left and whimpered. "I have to go see Cecily."

"Did we get the account?"

Megan glanced up at her eager receptionist. She swallowed. "Not yet. I'm still working on it."

Jennifer grinned and gave an admiring shake of her head. "It must be looking good if he stopped by himself."

"It definitely has potential," Megan agreed. Huge potential. But Collin? She mentally shook her head. There was getting creative, and then there was moving mountains.

Collin was the Rockies.

* * *

"So, what are his weaknesses?" asked Cecily as she cut through the side seam of the jacket she was altering on the sewing table of her shop, Well Suited.

"He's closed-minded and pigheaded," said Megan, hopping up to sit on the counter that ran below the front window of the store.

"Anything else?"

Megan thought about it. "He has a weakness for puppies."

"Too bad Victor isn't a puppy."

Megan laughed darkly. "We'd probably have a better chance of getting him to endorse dogfood."

"O'Patrick Chow," laughed Cecily, cutting away. "All natural, organically grown, fifteen vitamins and minerals—"

"Proceeds go to the homeless shelter for puppies," Megan put in.

Cecily stopped cutting. "That's it."

Megan frowned. "That can't be it. Ferretti Industries doesn't have a pet food division."

"No. Proceeds. Proceeds to go to…who? What? Where? What would Collin support?"

"Besides dogs?" Megan bit her bottom lip. "Cats? Mice? Gophers?" She paused. "Panthers!"

"Ferretti makes panther food?"

"No, no. I mean, kids. Soccer players. Minor soccer. Anna's team is named the *Panthers*."

Cecily grinned. "There you go. Take a good, long look at Ferretti's business interests and find out how they're linked into kids' soccer."

"Oh, man…" Megan hopped down from the counter, her mind starting to hum as she paced across the shop. "Yeah. It's good. But I have to be subtle."

She flipped her hair back from her forehead. "We can't just come right out and tell Collin we want his endorsement. We need to schmooze him, massage him, make sure he understands just how good the cause is…"

"You go, Ms. Advertising Executive," said Cecily.

Megan pulled Cecily into a quick hug. "You're a genius."

"Tell that to my customers."

"I do. Every Tuesday night on the radio show."

"If I'm such a genius, why can't I understand this?" asked Cecily several hours later when she was curled up on Megan's couch sipping a mug of sweet coffee.

"It's simple," Megan responded, dropping Ferretti's last year's annual report onto her coffee table and crossing her legs beneath her in the worn armchair.

She leaned forward, cradling her own mug. "Ferretti Industries made a five-thousand-dollar donation to Mile High Soccer Academy for children last year."

"And…?" asked Cecily.

"You said it yourself. We use Collin's weakness. He has a soft spot for soccer kids."

"If it was that easy, he'd have endorsed about a million athletic products by now."

Megan pointed to the open newspaper. "That's where the auction comes in. We convince Collin he needs to go into the auction to help the kids."

Cecily smirked. "After dating you, I don't think he'll be willing to sell himself to the highest bidder, even if it is for a good cause."

"Hey!"

Cecily laughed.

Megan crossed her arms over her chest. "He won't have to go on a date."

"It's a celebrity auction. What else is anybody going to do with him?"

"Play soccer."

"Oh, yeah. I can see it all now. Rich widows from Cherry Creek, pushing up the bidding for a chance to play soccer with sexy Collin O'Patrick."

"That's the beauty of it. We auction off a soccer clinic featuring Collin O'Patrick and eighteen free tickets to the next Peaks game. Parents will buy it for their kids. Think of what a great birthday party it would make. And Victor will bid on it because he likes soccer and he likes kids, and it's going to benefit the academy. Honestly, Cecily, I could not have dreamed up a better opportunity myself."

"And Collin's going to agree to be a celebrity prize because…?"

Megan had already thought about that. "Because I'll ask him while he's naked."

"Planning to get naked with him again soon."

"Absolutely."

Cecily's eyes glimmered. "That part's definitely going to work."

"Thank you."

"Okay. So you're naked. And he says yes. And you

go to the auction. This convinces Collin to endorse Ferretti Industries because…?"

"Because I arrange, in advance, for Victor McKnight to bid at the auction and donate Collin and the clinic to a worthy team."

"You're going to fix an auction?"

"No, I'm going to tell Victor McKnight to keep bidding."

"What if he doesn't?"

"Why wouldn't he?"

"What if the bids get too high?"

"Ferretti is a corporation, Cecily. What set of parents can afford to outbid them for a birthday party?"

"Hmm," said Cecily, sitting back and taking another sip of her coffee.

"There's no hmm about it." It was a great plan. A brilliant plan. A damn near perfect plan. "At the end of it all, Ferretti looks like a fabulous corporate citizen, Victor McKnight gets a chance to schmooze Collin, a deserving team gets a free clinic and soccer game, and the academy gets a donation."

"And you get?"

"The contract of a freaking lifetime."

"What if you get caught?"

"Get caught how? At what? Ferretti already supports the academy. It's not the least bit strange that they'd do it again."

Cecily shook her head. "I don't know…"

"You worry too much."

"So, after the auction, Collin is so impressed by the

generosity of Ferretti Industries that he spontaneously offers to endorse their products?"

Megan bit down on her polished thumbnail. "This is only phase one."

"What's phase two?"

"I haven't figured that out yet."

Cecily raised her eyebrows. "Don't you think you should figure out the *entire* plan before you plunge in with both feet?"

"I can't."

"Why not?"

"The auction is Sunday afternoon."

Collin stared across the softly lit hot tub to where Megan's head and shoulders were silhouetted against the stars. "I did something really, really awful in a previous life, didn't I?"

She gave him a shiny, sexy smile that made his muscles flex despite the fact that they'd just made love. "Don't be so melodramatic. It'll be fun."

"Fun, my ass." He took a swig of his Beaujolais.

She wiggled her hands through the bubbling water. The submerged lights gave her pale body a sensual glow.

"It's for a good cause," she pointed out in a soft voice. "The academy offers clinics for ages eight to eighteen. They have four regulation soccer fields. The money they're raising is to finish the fifth one."

He dragged his gaze from the opaque view of her body, focusing on her face, hoping that would help him keep his perspective. It didn't. Her jewel eyes were as bad as her perfect breasts. "I'll write a check."

She slowly slid along the bench until she was lightly brushing against him with the movement of the water. "Collin," she sing-songed in a voice that let him know she was deeply disappointed.

He sighed. "This is cheating."

"Cheating how?" she all but purred in his ear.

He lifted one arm out of the warm water and stretched it across the edge of the tub. "You are offering me a bribe, Ms. Brock."

"How so? I just gave you everything I had."

Despite himself, he smiled at the memory. She might be exasperating as hell, but she was also the cutest, sexiest woman he'd ever come across. "You offering it all again?"

There was a smile in her voice. "All of it?"

He wrapped his arm around her wet shoulders, sliding his fingertips along the satin skin of her collarbone. "Can't think of anything *I'd* leave out."

She snuggled down against him, and he kissed her temple.

"This is not a bribe," she said.

"Oh, it's a bribe, all right."

She shook her head. "You just have to decide whether or not to make eighteen sweet children deliriously happy and support a good cause, or be a poop."

"You know how I feel about public appearances."

"This is hardly public. If you're expecting more news

helicopters hovering overhead, I think you've overestimated your popularity."

He chuckled at that, kissing the back of her neck. "You think I'm conceited?"

"I think you're misguided."

He combed her wet hair back from her forehead. "I think you're gorgeous."

"Did I mention top coaches? Certified referees?"

"I believe you did."

Her voice turned breathy as her fingertips trailed their way across his chest. "Training videos? Scrimmage games? Written evaluations?"

He zeroed in on her earlobe, taking the soft flesh between his lips. "Got it," he mumbled.

"And a free T-shirt?"

He drew back. "Hell, for a free T-shirt…"

She tipped her head sideways. "Are you agreeing?"

He slid her into his lap, letting his gaze wander down to her bare breasts. Seconds later, his hand trailed down the same path. He kissed her, long and hard and deeply.

"Collin?" she murmured.

"I don't suppose we can talk about this later?"

"Are you kidding?"

"Fine. Yes." Yes to the auction. Yes to the academy. Yes to holding her. Yes to kissing her. Yes to loving her.

Whoa. Wait. Back up. They weren't there yet.

He drew away to look into her soft green eyes. But they were getting damn close.

She stared at him for a long minute, finally breathing his name on the night air.

He reached up to place one palm against her cheek, sobering. "This is about to get really complicated," he warned.

She didn't react to his mood change. "Actually, I read the brochure. It'll be quite simple."

He gave up and chuckled low. Then he tipped his forehead to touch hers. "Nothing that has anything to do with you is simple."

She placed a soft kiss on his mouth, and his heart contracted.

"In a good way?" she asked.

"Jury's still out on that one."

He might well be the happiest man on the planet right now. But he was coherent enough to recognize trouble when it climbed into his lap. He was already doing everything *her way*. Could blender drinks and talking about his feelings be far behind?

Maybe Megan was right. Maybe he did have an inflated ego. Certainly, nobody at Marshall's Auction House was paying any undue attention to him. Here he was merely one of more than a dozen sports figures and celebrities who'd agreed to auction off some of their time to aid the Mile High Soccer Academy.

They were midway through the afternoon, and tens of thousands of dollars had been raised. Collin had to admit, he got an emotional kick out of being part of the event.

Megan sat in a chair next to him in the second row. He took her hand from her lap and gave it a squeeze.

She turned to look at him and smiled while the bidding for a professional football player went over the five-thousand-dollar mark. The player stood next to the podium hamming it up and encouraging the bidders to go higher.

She leaned toward Collin. "See? It's not so bad."

Collin put his lips next to her ear. "I'll survive. But I'm thinking you need to bribe me again later."

She pulled away and gave him an admonishing look, but the sparkle in her eyes told him his chances were good.

"Busy for dinner?" he muttered.

"Pay attention."

"I'm just sayin', if you're not busy later, maybe I could throw a couple of steaks on the barbecue."

"I have to work tomorrow."

"I have practice."

"I can't stay over again."

"Nobody invited you." Yeah. Right. Like he'd ever say no to her company in his bed.

She butted his shoulder with hers. "You trying to embarrass me?"

"I'm the one who has to get up on stage."

"You'll love it."

"I don't think so."

The hammer in the auctioneer's hand came down. "Sold. To the gentleman in the third row."

Megan and Collin joined in with the applause.

"Next up, we have Denver Peaks soccer player, Collin O'Patrick."

Collin's stomach contracted as the audience applauded the announcement.

Megan gave his arm a squeeze. "Go get 'em, jungle cat."

He shot her an exasperated look.

She laughed.

"Mr. O'Patrick is offering a two-hour soccer clinic and eighteen tickets to his next home game," said the auctioneer.

Collin mounted the steps to the stage, surprised that the clapping wasn't dying down.

The auctioneer stepped back from the podium and motioned for Collin to approach.

As the other participants had done, Collin walked up to the microphone to give a brief speech.

"Good afternoon, ladies and gentlemen," he began.

The cheering went on a little longer.

He stood there, feeling ridiculously self-conscious. It wasn't that he'd never spoken in front of a crowd before, but he was uncomfortable with their enthusiasm. And who wanted to be bid on? If the price was too low, it could be really embarrassing.

He tried again, hoping to get this over with quickly. "Thank you all very much for coming out to support the Mile High Soccer Academy this afternoon."

The applause finally died down.

He motioned to the auctioneer. "As the announcer said, I'm offering a two-hour clinic for a soccer team. I'm flexible about the format. I can work in conjunction with the coach to meet the team's needs, and hopefully help them develop a little bit. Thank you."

He stepped back.

The auctioneer shook his hand and stepped up to the podium, wooden gavel in hand. "Shall we start the bidding at a thousand?

"I've got a thousand. Two. Three." He pointed at the crowd with the handle of his gavel. "Four over there. Five. Six."

Collin peered at the crowd, trying to figure out who was bidding. Was the announcer sure somebody had said six-thousand dollars? For two hours?

"Do I hear seven? Six five? I have six five. I have seven. Can I get seven five? Yes. Seven five, there in the corner."

Collin couldn't believe it. He was setting the record for the day. What kind of a lunatic spent so much on a soccer clinic? Quite frankly, he didn't know *anything* that was worth seven thousand five hundred dollars.

"Is that eight, ma'am? I have eight. Can I get nine? Nine? Nine. I have nine."

Collin wanted to tell them to stop. He caught Megan's eyes and she gave him a wide grin and a thumbs up.

Of course she did. The woman had a mercenary soul.

Okay, so it was for a good cause. Still…

"I have nine. Do I hear nine five? Anybody?"

Collin breathed a sigh of relief. Another few seconds, and it would be over. Once he was on the field with the kids, he knew he'd enjoy himself. He just had to make it through the next—

"I have nine five. I have ten. I have ten five. I have eleven."

Collin nearly staggered back.

"Eleven thousand, going once… Is that twelve?" Twelve thousand. Do I hear thirteen?"

The room went silent.

Collin stopped breathing.

The auctioneer held the gavel poised over the desk for a second, two, three.

Bang.

"Sold to the gentleman in the first row for twelve thousand dollars."

The crowd cheered once again, and a man in the first row stood up while an auction worker handed him some papers on a clipboard.

Collin took a deep breath. Following the lead of those that went before him, he headed down the stairs to thank the successful bidder.

The man handed the pen back to the auction worker, turned to Collin and stuck out his hand. "Victor McKnight, Ferretti Industries."

Collin shook. "That was a very generous bid."

"You and I have a mutual interest in kids' soccer. Mind if we get a picture?" Victor gestured behind Collin.

Collin hid his surprise. "Sure. Uh. No problem."

They smiled and shook hands for the camera.

CHAPTER ELEVEN

FRIDAY night and Megan knew she was running out of time.

It had been five days since Collin had set a record at the celebrity auction and made page one of the sports section.

Victor was getting impatient.

Megan had put the man off again this morning by telling him that she'd definitely sign Collin up tonight. And she was going to.

"Should we go to Maddigo's?" asked Collin as he let Rocky in through the back door.

Rocky immediately scampered across the living room and hopped up on Megan's lap. She stroked his head, and he rolled over, all but begging for her to scratch his tummy. His unbridled adoration calmed her fluttering nerves.

Collin leaned sideways against the door jamb between the kitchen and living room, folding his arms over his chest. "You're spoiling him, you know."

She patted Rocky's plump stomach. "He's just a baby. He needs love and attention."

"So do I."

"You're a big boy."

Collin crossed the room and took the opposite end of the couch, angling his body toward her. "When he weighs eighty pounds, you're going to regret letting him get used to your lap. You want to eat in or out?"

"In," she said. Where they could talk. Where she could make the best pitch possible for Ferretti Industries.

"Don't want to leave baby Rocky alone?" Collin teased.

"Hey, you're a bigger sap than I am. You brought him home."

"So why does he love you better?"

"Because I'm inherently lovable."

Collin didn't answer, but his eyes got all soft and sweet, and she knew she had to get the Ferretti pitch out of the way so they could get on with their relationship.

If he said yes, he said yes. She'd make sure he never regretted it.

If he said no, she'd accept that. She'd never completely understand his rationale, but she'd respect his decision.

"You want wine?" He started to rise.

"Hang on a sec."

"What?" He sat back down.

She took a deep breath, mentally rehearsing all the catch-phrases she'd come up with. "Collin. There's something we—"

The front doorbell rang.

He didn't move. "Is everything okay?"

She shook her head. "It's fine."

He stared at her intently, a very serious expression on his face. "You and me?"

"We're good."

The doorbell rang again.

He squinted at her. "You sure. You weren't about to break up with me, were you?"

Was there something to break up here? Had they gone that far? A warm, secure sensation settled in her chest.

Maybe they had.

She smiled at him, shaking her head again. "No."

He still didn't move, monitoring her expression.

"I promise," she said. "This isn't the 'let's just be friends' speech." She looked down, giving Rocky's tummy a hearty scratch as she went out on an emotional limb. "I'm going to be around when this guy weighs eighty pounds, remember?"

"Good."

The doorbell rang for a third time.

"You should really answer the door."

He stood up. "Okay. As long as we're good."

Megan took a deep breath that filled her chest. "We're good."

He nodded sharply in apparent satisfaction and headed for the door.

"Collin!" It was Anna's voice.

Megan craned her neck and saw Anna rush through the doorway and throw her arms around Collin. "I love you!"

Collin was propelled a step backward while his arms went loosely around Anna's back. "Whoa," he said. "You're going to make Megan jealous here."

Brett stepped in behind Anna. "Forget Megan. She's making *me* jealous."

"Hey, Brett," Megan called from the couch, laughter lacing her voice. "Wanna pull your girlfriend off Collin?"

Anna drew back, hands still on Collin's upper arms. "You are the sweetest, the *sweetest* man in the entire world."

Brett cleared his throat.

Collin cocked his head toward Megan. "You hear that?"

She waved her hand in dismissal. "She's a soccer player. They're a little loony."

All three heads turned to pin her with incredulous stares.

"Oh, get over yourselves," she said.

"So, what did I do to deserve your undying adoration this month?" Collin asked Anna.

"Victor McKnight just called."

Megan froze as the blood drained from her face. Her hand tightened convulsively, and Rocky wiggled in protest.

"Who's Victor McKnight?" asked Collin. "A soccer scout?"

"No," Anna answered as Brett wrapped one arm around her stomach and pulled her back against him.

"That's better," he grunted.

Megan held her breath.

"Victor McKnight is the guy from Ferretti Industries," said Anna. "You know. The one who bought your clinic and soccer tickets."

"Oh, that guy. Why'd he call you?"

"To offer the clinic to the Panthers. We've got you

for two solid hours at the Mile High tomorrow, O'Patrick, and we're gonna run you ragged."

"Your brats?" asked Collin with a twinkle in his eye.

Megan let out her breath. Giving the Panthers the clinic was probably overkill on Victor's part, but at least he hadn't preempted Megan's conversation with Collin.

"My brats," said Anna with a lilt to her voice.

"Brett's helping," Collin stated.

"Hey? How'd I get dragged into this."

"Simple. You have to show an interest in her career. It's on the list. We're ordering in. You guys wanna hang out for a while?"

"The list?" asked Brett, moving with Anna toward the living room. "Since when did we start paying any attention to the list?"

Anna elbowed him in the stomach. "Since you started doing things *my way*."

"No point in fighting it," said Collin with a deep sigh of resignation.

Megan grinned at the mock disgust on his face.

It was midnight before Anna and Brett made it back out the door.

As soon as they were gone Collin pulled Megan into his arms, pressing her up against the wall of the entryway. "Since you're not breaking up with me..." He gave her a long, drawn-out kiss. "Wanna sleep over?"

"Sure." Good idea. If she stayed over, they'd have plenty of time to talk before morning. Plenty of time for her to make her case.

"I think Rocky's out for the night." Collin kissed her again. "You're all mine."

"Collin, we have to—"

He cut her off with another kiss. This one had her knees going weak, and her heart rate speeding up, and her arms creeping around his neck.

"Collin, we…" she moaned, weaker this time.

His hand slipped under her T-shirt, his rough fingers closing around one breast. His voice rasped against her ear. "It's Friday night. You're all liquored up on fine wine. And I've been lusting after you since eight o'clock. So unless you're breaking up with me, telling me you're secretly married, secretly engaged or not in the mood, it can wait until morning."

His fingertips surrounded one nipple, and a groan escaped from her lips.

"Cross not-in-the-mood off the list," he whispered, drawing her in for another long kiss, pressing his muscular body against her curves.

Megan gave up. She loved his kisses, loved his hands, loved every single inch of his body. She wanted him naked. Now.

The conversation could wait until tomorrow. She'd debate better sober anyway.

Collin stared at Megan in the morning light. She was fast asleep in his bed, her head cradled by his pillow, gorgeous, blonde hair fanned out like a halo. She looked perfect right there.

He'd waited as long as he dared before leaving for

the soccer clinic, half hoping she'd wake up, half hoping he'd get to leave her there sleeping.

Maybe she'd stay.

Maybe she'd be here when he got back, playing with Rocky, hanging out in his bathrobe, watching his television. Maybe she'd even bake cookies in his kitchen.

He shook his head at the absurd twist to his fantasy then bent over to give her a goodbye kiss on the forehead.

She sighed in her sleep, but her eyes didn't open.

He smoothed back her hair, inhaling deeply and, filling his lungs with her sweet scent. Then he straightened and smiled. He knew he was falling fast and hard, but he cared less and less with each passing hour.

Collin let himself out of the house and cruised along the quiet Denver streets. It was a route he'd taken a thousand times, but he'd never noticed the oak trees, the bird houses, the kids' bikes and the flower gardens. It was a friendly neighborhood, a family neighborhood, and he had a wonderful woman and the cutest dog in the world tucked away in his house.

He made it to the academy half an hour before the clinic was due to start.

A couple of the girls were already out on one of the smoothly trimmed fields passing a ball between them. They waved a greeting, and he waved back.

He tossed his athletic bag behind the bench and stripped off his sweats. While he was lacing up his cleats, a man strode down the side of the field toward him.

The man approached and held out his hand. "Scott Parker. I'm the Chancellor of Mile High."

"Collin O'Patrick."

Scott grinned. "I know who you are. This field okay with you?"

Collin nodded. "Seems fine."

"Anything you need?"

Collin gazed out into the field again. "Looks like the girls found some balls."

"Extra balls, pinnies, cones, whatever you need will be in the equipment shack on the sidelines. It's unlocked. I can give you an equipment runner if you need it."

Collin grinned and shook his head. "The girls can do the running. Good practice for them."

"We've got twelve-year-old boys in camp this week. They're due on the fields in half an hour or so. I suspect some of them may turn into an audience."

"No problem," said Collin.

"The cameras are due at ten," said Scott.

Collin's eyebrows flexed. "Cameras."

"Victor McKnight is taking some publicity shots."

"Can he do that?"

"I gave him my permission. You can refuse, of course. But since he spent twelve thousand dollars on this gig, I was inclined to cut him some slack."

Collin wasn't thrilled at the prospect of being in any more publicity shots, but twelve thousand dollars was one heck of a big charitable donation.

"Fine," he said to Scott.

"You sure?"

"No problem. Just make sure he gets the girls'

parents to sign releases. I'm not putting any teenagers out in public without permission."

"Definitely," Scott agreed.

Anna's voice rang from across the field where more and more girls had joined in the passing game. "Ready to run hard, O'Patrick?"

"You're late," Collin called back.

"I'm rested," she replied.

"Let me know if you need anything," said Scott, taking his leave.

"Thanks." Collin turned his attention to Anna. "Glad you had a good, long sleep. We're starting with wind sprints."

"I'll coach from the sidelines."

"You'll run with the girls."

"You're a hard-ass."

"Where's Brett?"

"He might be late. He was in the shower when I left."

"So you lied about getting a good night's sleep."

Anna grinned. "I'm not doing any wind sprints."

Collin laughed as he headed out onto the field. "Why do I have the feeling Brett's going to side with you?"

They worked on drills for the first hour, and then moved into a scrimmage game. As Scott had predicted, the twelve-year-old boys began trickling over to watch. Collin nabbed a few and put them on a team. Soon they had two full teams, each a mix of seventeen-year-old girls and twelve-year-old boys.

He was refereeing at center field when he saw Megan

arrive on the far sideline. He gave her a wave before blowing down an out-of-bounds pass.

The players quickly set up for the throw-in, while the photographer snapped a few shots. Then he headed back to his mountain of equipment on the sidelines. The boys were clearly thrilled to be included, and the presence of the photographer simply added to the excitement of the morning.

As the play went on Collin jogged over to Brett. "Call Coach and get us twenty more tickets for tonight's game."

Brett grinned. "You're such a soft touch."

"Hey, the kids are having a blast." Collin would feel like a jerk if he couldn't invite all of them to the game.

Anna approached. "Somebody here to talk to you."

Collin watched the play as he spoke. *"Now?"*

"The guy who paid the twelve grand," said Anna. "I can ref for a minute."

"Probably wants another picture," Collin muttered, pulling the whistle over his head and handing it to Anna.

"That's what you get for being a celebrity."

"Don't even joke about it."

"Did you see Megan was here?"

Collin gazed across to the far side of the field again. She was pretty small over there near the parking lot, but it was enough to know she'd come to see him.

Leaving Anna in charge, he trotted over to Victor McKnight and the photographer.

"Nice to see you again, Collin," said Victor with a

hearty slap on the back. "Did you talk to Megan last night?"

Collin drew back. What the hell did Megan have to do with anything?

Victor waited.

"Uh. Yeah," Collin answered slowly. "We talked."

"Good." Another back slap.

Okay. Collin gestured to the photographer, hoping to get back to the game as soon as possible. "Did you want a picture or something?"

"So everything is set?"

Set for what? The clinic was under way. The tickets were arranged. They'd taken enough pictures to fill ten photo albums.

"It's fine," said Collin. "The picture…"

Victor stuck out his hand again. "Welcome aboard, Collin. I can guarantee you won't be sorry. Megan and I have an entire endorsement campaign worked—"

"You and *Megan*?" Collin asked, his stomach turning to lead.

"Megan," said Victor.

"Megan Brock?" Collin glanced across the field in disbelief. Campaign? Endorsement?

"Of course, Megan Brock. Wouldn't take the account away from her now. Not after landing you. She's a little trooper, that girl."

Megan felt Collin's stare.

She squinted, confused. He was a long way away, but his posture seemed almost…angry.

She blinked and leaned forward.

His shoulders were squared, his arms folded over his chest, head cocked to one side, as he talked to…Victor?

Her knees nearly collapsed as panic winged its way through her brain.

Collin was talking to *Victor*. And Victor had expected Megan to settle things with Collin last night.

She staggered onto the field, intent on getting to them as quickly as possible.

Her walk turned into a jog, then into a run.

Soccer players rushed around her and the ball whooshed over her head.

Anna called her name, but she ignored the shout.

She had to get to them. She had to stop the conversation. If she didn't shut this down in the next thirty seconds, both her personal and professional lives were going to be completely destroyed.

A few of the players had to run around her. A couple stopped to watch her. But she finally cleared the center of the field and made her way toward Collin and Victor.

When she arrived, legs burning and lungs laboring, Collin was shaking Victor's hand. "There's obviously been some sort of confusion," he said. "I'll call you on Monday and we can clear it up."

Megan opened her mouth, but the long run had robbed her of the ability to speak.

Victor looked at her quizzically as Collin's arm clamped like steel around her shoulders.

He pivoted and marched her down the sidelines away from Victor.

She sucked in gulps of air, still unable to speak, wishing Collin would say something.

What had happened? What had Victor said? How could she fix it? *How* was she supposed to mount a defense when she didn't know anything?

"I have five minutes left in this clinic," Collin finally hissed in her ear. He stopped well away from the rest of the crowd. "Don't you move."

"Collin," she gasped, regaining her voice.

"Don't." He held up an admonishing finger.

"But—"

"No." His steel eyes burned into hers.

She swallowed.

The whistle sounded to end the scrimmage.

Collin stared at her for a long second, then he turned and walked away.

Megan sank down on the lush grass, dropping her forehead onto her knees.

Collin obviously knew about the ad campaign. She was never going to talk him into it now. And Victor was going to lose all confidence in her. He'd probably never deal with her again.

She should have talked to Collin last night. Even though it had been late. Even though he was sweet and sexy and she'd wanted to make love with him so bad, she should have made him listen to her pitch.

"Megan?" His voice interrupted her frantic thoughts.

She looked up. The others were making their way off the field.

"I can explain," she said weakly.

"You don't need to," he answered.

Wait a minute. That was encouraging.

She slowly rose to her feet, voice hesitant and searching. "You understand?"

His expression was like granite, his eyes like steel and his voice dripped icicles. "Perfectly."

Uh oh. He obviously didn't understand what she wanted him to understand.

"Collin—"

"Why?"

"Why did I want you to do an ad campaign?"

"Why did you lie to me?"

"I didn't—"

He laughed coldly, raking his hand through his short hair. "You and your high and mighty bastion of perfection—"

"I didn't *lie* to you."

The field was now clear, and his voice rose. "The radio show. The newspaper. The auction. The clinic. My God, you slept with me, planning to sell me to the *highest bidder*."

"I *never*—"

"And you dare to criticize *men*?"

"Collin." Megan reached out to touch his arm. She had to make him listen. Their personal relationship had nothing to do with Ferretti Industries. "You don't understand."

He shook off her hand, and his voice dropped to a harsh, uncompromising growl. "Oh, I understand all right."

"Collin—"

"I let you past the façade, and you *played* me."

His words sent a shock wave through her brain, robbing her of the power of speech. She staggered back.

His eyes turned bleak as ice, and he swore out loud. He stared at her for a moment with disgust before shaking his head and turning away.

She opened her mouth to call after him, to defend herself, but no sound came out.

Played him?

She hadn't…

Had she?

CHAPTER TWELVE

MEGAN clicked Cecily's front door shut behind her and leaned heavily back against it. Her stomach was a giant ball of lead, and there was a sharp pain stabbing through the center of her chest.

Cecily looked up from her sketchpad. "What?"

Megan shook her head, afraid her voice might crack if she tried to talk. *What* had she done?

Cecily stood. "What's wrong? What happened?"

"Collin," Megan whispered.

"Is he okay?"

Megan nodded and drew in a ragged breath, trying to put on a brave face for Cecily. She didn't want anybody to know how badly she'd screwed up. "He's okay."

Cecily paused. "But?"

Megan forced a laugh. "But I think he's probably taking out a hit on me."

Cecily crossed the floor, brow furrowing as she peered into Megan's eyes. "What did you do?"

"Victor got to him before I did."

Cecily hesitated again. "Oh, Megan. I'd be totally

sympathetic if I had any idea what you were talking about." There was a teasing twinkle in her eye.

Megan gave a weak chuckle. Then she scrunched her eyes shut and pushed the heels of her palms against them. She tried unsuccessfully to block out the memory of Collin's expression as he'd tossed out his accusations. "Victor told Collin about the endorsement deal before I could do it."

"Uh oh."

Megan dropped her hands and straightened away from the door. "Yeah. I blew it, Cecily. Big time."

Cecily cursed, and the twinkle went out of her eyes.

"It's over," said Megan. "And it's nobody's fault but mine."

"Did you talk to him?"

Megan nodded. "He thinks I lied to him. He thinks sleeping with him was all part of a big plot to get the Ferretti contract. He thinks I set him up from day one."

"Did you?"

"Of *course* not."

"Is it too early for margaritas?"

Megan slumped down on the couch, suddenly exhausted. "It's gotta be five o'clock somewhere in the world."

Cecily headed for the kitchen. "What are you going to do?"

"There's nothing I can do."

"There's always something you can do."

"Not this time."

Her friend stood with her hand on the refrigerator

door. "Which do you want to fight for: the contract or the man?"

"They're both gone."

"But if you had to pick. Which would you choose?"

Megan pushed back her hair, thinking about it. "The contract's nothing." She gave a cold laugh. "You know, I was going to give him my best pitch. But I was willing to accept it if he said no. I figured I'd ask, lay the logic on the table, and if he didn't want to do it, I'd…"

"Keep sleeping with him anyway?"

"Yes. Yes! Hell, I was planning his dog's future."

Cecily dumped the ice cubes into the blender. "Do you love him?"

What a question.

When she didn't answer, Cecily continued. "Are you alive when he's there, only half focused when he's not?"

Was she?

"Do you think about him all the time? Does your heart give a little jump when he comes into the room?"

Megan closed her eyes. This was sounding frighteningly familiar.

"Did a light go out when he walked away?" Cecily asked softly.

Yes. Damn it. The light was gone, and it wasn't coming back.

"You love him," said Cecily.

Megan gave a harsh laugh. "Not much point in loving him anymore."

"But you do."

Megan's shoulders slumped in sheer exhaustion. "Do you think we were wrong?"

"Wrong about what?"

"Wrong about the list? Collin has this thing about seeing the 'real person'—"

Cecily sighed deeply.

"He thinks our list is full of manipulative tricks."

Cecily's finger hovered over the blender button. "I think our list is full of kindness and generosity. We say we want men who are interested in our career. That doesn't mean we won't be interested in theirs. We want men who'll bring flowers. That doesn't mean we won't do nice things for them."

"Is Collin wrong, then?"

"Sad truth is, there are more jerks out there than nice guys. If a guy can't see his way clear to make the woman he loves a blender drink when times are good, then what the hell else won't he do for her when times are bad? It's about respect and love and support." Cecily hit the button and noise filled the room.

Cecily was right. She was smart, and she was right.

But Collin was right, too.

If two people wanted a relationship to work, they had to be up front with each other. She might not have tried to coerce him with sex, but she'd misled him about the auction. She'd tried to manipulate his emotions so he'd see things her way. And she'd never, not once, let him see all the way down to her soul.

Because the deep-down truth was, she was tough, and she was driven, and sometimes she convinced herself that the end justified the means. It wasn't a pretty picture down there.

Odds were, Collin could never love her soul.

She was a façade, and he deserved better.

So did Victor McKnight.

Without stopping to give herself time to think, Megan pulled out Victor's business card and dialed his private cell phone number.

The sound of the blender died as the ring tones filled her ear.

"McKnight here," he answered.

"Mr. McKnight?"

"Yes."

"This is Megan Brock."

His voice stayed crisp and professional. "Megan. I wanted to—"

"I'm calling to apologize, Mr. McKnight. You counted on me, and I let you down. I can no longer hope to represent Collin O'Patrick. The contract is dead, which means the Anna Simpson deal is dead, too. I will, of course, fulfill my obligations for the baby-food division. But, after that, I'll consider our business relationship at an end."

"Megan, I can't see why you—"

"I'm sorry. This is a difficult call for me to make. I hope you understand that I have to say goodbye." Guilt and remorse had her voice cracking on the last word. She quickly hung up the phone.

Cecily stared silently from the kitchen, a margarita in each hand.

Megan gritted her teeth and squared her shoulders. As usual, a good margarita would have to make up for a whole lot of pain.

This wasn't the worst thing that had ever happened to her. She'd survive. Somehow.

"There are worse things in the world than making television commercials," Brett said to Collin as the two of them sat side by side during the halftime break.

"Name one," said Collin. His chest was raw, his anger fresh, his skin practically jumped with contained energy. He wished the damn whistle would blow so he could get back out there and run until his mind was blank.

"Flood, fire and pestilence."

Collin grunted.

Brett jabbed his thumb at the stands behind him, where nearly forty young fans had prime seats thanks to the auction and the generosity of the Peaks' coach. "Kids who wouldn't otherwise get to see a professional soccer game. You did a good thing, O'Patrick."

"I was duped."

"Are you pissed or embarrassed?"

"I'm pissed."

"Pissed because you contributed to a worthy cause?"

"Pissed because Megan lied to me."

"She didn't lie to you. She pulled one over on you, and you can't stand it."

"I trusted her, and she played me."

"She didn't tell you about the auction because she was afraid you'd be unreasonable about it."

"She didn't tell me about the auction because she wanted to con me into endorsing Ferretti Industries."

"And that's such an unforgivable crime?"

Collin glanced at the referee. Where the hell was the whistle?

"Did you even talk to the guy?" asked Brett.

"What guy?"

"McKnight. Do you even know what she negotiated?"

"I'm not endorsing commercial products."

"Why not?"

"We've had this conversation before."

"Look down at your shoes."

"Go to hell."

"Look down. They're Ferrettis. They're not Coopers, not Blanchard's, not Longchamp. They're Ferrettis."

"And your point is?"

"You buy them because they're good. I buy them because they're good. What the hell is so wrong with saying that to the world?"

"I don't have to justify my decision to you."

"I talked to McKnight."

Collin turned to glare at Brett. "You *what*?"

"I talked to the guy. I asked him what he was offering you. Do you know what he said?"

"I don't care."

"Megan got him to agree that you can endorse or not endorse any product you want. They will go over every detail with you from materials to union agreements with the subcontractors to make sure you're comfortable with it. You have veto power over the commercials, and a percent of gross—*gross*, not net—goes to children's soccer."

Collin gritted his teeth. Brett had absolutely no business talking to anyone about anything on his behalf.

"Collin. I'm your friend. We don't always agree, but I've always respected you. You and Megan have had this contest thing going on for weeks now. She came out on top today. She was smarter than you. Or maybe her judgment was less clouded than yours—"

"There is nothing wrong with my judgment."

Brett laughed. "You're in love with the woman. You can't see straight for wanting her. Trust me. I know what I'm talking about."

"She was wrong," said Collin.

"She was smart. Ferretti offered you the deal of a lifetime, and she was trying to help you make a good decision—"

"She only wanted the commission."

Brett paused, and Collin realized that logic sounded weak even to him.

Damn. He didn't want to let go of his anger just yet. She was wrong and he was right.

"Yeah," Brett drawled after a moment, nodding. "Right. Megan's always struck me as the mercenary type."

"You don't know her like I do." Collin wasn't about to admit out loud that the mercenary argument rang a little hollow now that he'd gotten to know her.

"That's because you're one lucky son of a bitch," said Brett.

"Hey, you've got Anna."

"Doesn't mean I don't know that Megan's a babe. Ask me, you're lucky she gave you the time of day."

"I don't feel particularly lucky."

"Ever stop to think she might have had your best interests at heart?"

"Nope."

"You look back at those kids and tell me you don't feel good about contributing to their soccer development. You tell me that you wouldn't feel good about putting thousands of dollars a year into minor sports programs. You tell me—"

"You ever considered running for office?"

"Am I getting to you?"

"No. You're pissing me off," Collin lied.

Truth was, Brett was getting to him. Somehow Megan's behavior didn't seem quite so reprehensible anymore. Yeah, she'd misled him, but that didn't necessarily mean she had sinister motives.

She might have been misguided, maybe mistaken. Maybe she honestly thought the endorsement contract was a good idea.

Brett stood up and stretched his arms above his head. "Did you know that McKnight agreed to offer Anna and the Panthers a contract if Megan could deliver you?"

Collin jerked his head to look up at Brett.

"Yeah, buddy. She negotiated you a dream deal, got money to support the Panthers tossed into the bargain, made some kids deliriously happy and got a twelve-thousand-dollar donation to Mile High Academy. I can see why you'd want to show her the door. Especially considering she's lazy, butt-ugly, with no sense of humor and the IQ of a gnat."

Brett slapped him on the shoulder. "Good move."

The referee's whistle blew, covering Collin's string of self-deprecating swear words.

Megan reached for the telephone in her apartment, swore under her breath, then put it back down again. She'd just finished talking to Cecily for the third time since she'd come home. It was too late to call Anna and apologize. And she couldn't, no matter how much she wanted to, phone Collin and try to explain one more time.

She reached for the television remote and clicked the power button. A cooking show appeared on her screen. There was no way Cornish game hen in plum sauce was going to take her mind off Collin, so she clicked to the next channel. A seventies sitcom. Nope. A horror movie. Next. A soccer game. Definitely not.

She hit the off button and scrunched her eyes shut, shuddering as she relived the force of Collin's anger—made even more powerful because he was right. Megan curled her hands into fists, concentrating on replacing the unsettling memory with a better one from this morning, when she'd woken up in Collin's bed to the sound of Rocky's nails on the kitchen floor.

Rocky had been playing with his rubber ball again, but he'd happily switched to trotting at her heels while she'd made herself a quick breakfast. Then she'd let him out in the yard for a run while she'd had a shower and got dressed. The whole time, she'd been anxious to get going, anxious to head for the academy and see Collin again.

She loved watching him out on the field, loved watching him run, kick the ball, shout instructions to the other players—looking fit and in control, covered with a sheen of sweat. Of course, when it came down to it, she loved pretty much anything he did.

But that was in the past.

She'd screwed up.

She'd focused on herself. Her wants. Her needs. Her, her, her. She punched her fist into a couch pillow.

Something rattled against her front door.

Trust Cecily to know when she needed comfort.

But why didn't she just walk right in?

Megan stood up and glanced down at her comfort clothes—her oldest sweats and the torn T-shirt. Much as she appreciated the concern, she didn't even want Cecily seeing her like this.

Still, it wasn't as if she could pretend she wasn't home. She blinked away the scratchy feeling in her eyes and crossed the room to open the door.

It was Collin.

She froze at the sight of him.

He gave her a crooked smile, holding up two glasses. "I made you a margarita."

Megan blinked.

"It's a blender drink," he offered.

She blinked again.

BARBARA DUNLOP   213

"Well, actually, I didn't really make it myself. Cecily made it for me. But I'm delivering it. Does that count?"

Megan opened her mouth, but the jumble in her brain hadn't sorted itself out into words.

"If you let me in," Collin continued, "I have a little surprise for you."

She shook herself, trying desperately to make sense of the situation. "But you're mad," she blurted out.

He shook his head, his smile turning reflective. "I got over it."

"But—"

"Can I come in? Our drinks are melting."

She took a shaky step back. "But I... But you..."

He turned to face her as she closed the door. "I'm sorry."

Megan shook her head. "No, *I'm* sorry. I should have told you. I shouldn't have lied—"

"You didn't lie."

"I planted Victor McKnight at the auction."

"I know. I talked to him."

She remembered the morning at the field. "I saw."

"No. Not then. It was—you mind if I put these things down?"

"Did you say Cecily made them?"

"Yeah."

Megan scooped one of the drinks out of his hand. "Then we should drink."

Collin cracked a smile. "She makes them that good?"

"No, she makes them that strong."

"Am I driving you to drink?" he asked.

"You're driving me—" She stopped and stared at him.

He was here. He was talking. He seemed as if he wanted to work things out. He'd brought her a *blender* drink.

Her knees suddenly felt weak, and she sank down into the armchair.

"You okay?" he asked.

"You brought me a blender drink."

He smiled and crouched down beside her. "Yeah."

"But I betrayed you."

"You did it for a good cause."

"But—"

He took her hand and rubbed his thumb across her palm. "With the exception of the auction setup, did I see the real you?"

She slowly nodded. Then she shook her head. "I'm a façade."

He smiled indulgently. "No, you're not."

"I'm mercenary. I put profit above everything."

"Then why did you give up the Ferretti account?"

"They were going to fire me."

"No, they weren't. You quit. You didn't even wait to see what they'd do."

"I didn't deserve it. I never deserved you."

"You quit because you felt guilty. Because you *don't* put profit above everything."

He was making her sound noble when she wasn't. Megan shook her head and took a drink. "Did Cecily tell you that?"

"McKnight told me that."

She cringed. "He contacted you again?"

"I contacted him."

"What do you mean?"

"I told him I'd do it."

"Do what?"

"The endorsements."

Megan's arm went weak, and her glass dropped to rest on her knee. She couldn't have heard him correctly. "You *what*?"

"I told him I'd do it, but only if you were part of the deal."

She searched his expression for signs that he was mocking or joking. "Why?"

Collin took her margarita and placed both drinks on the coffee table. Then he took her hands in his and stared into her eyes. "Before I answer that, am I right when I think there's an us?"

Her stomach turned over. "What do you mean?"

His expression turned completely serious. "No games, Megan. I just want to know. Is there an us?"

She nodded.

"And did you mean it when you said you wanted to be around when Rocky was eighty pounds?"

It was time for total honesty. "Yes."

He took a deep breath. "You probably know that I think bearing your soul to another person is the single most loving, most intimate, most important thing you can ever do."

Megan blinked at the sting in her eyes again. "I'm sor—"

He placed his fingertips across her lips. "Shh."

She stopped talking.

"I have a little surprise in my pocket," he said.

"Collin—"

"It's a risk."

"You don't need—"

"But I do need… I think I want to bare my soul."

A wave of emotion coursed through Megan. And it was her turn to put her finger over his lips.

This was her fault. Hers. She'd take the first risk, not him. She owed him that much. She loved him, and she was ready to bare her own soul. "Collin, I—"

"Never mind." He talked right over her fingers as if she hadn't even interrupted. "I've already decided. I decided while Cecily was making the margaritas."

He let go of Megan's hand and reached into his jacket pocket, pulling out a deep purple velvet box.

She froze. Her eyes went wide and her ears filled with the roar of a storm.

Collin popped open the box, and a huge solitaire winked up at her. Before she could react, he smoothly shifted so that he was on one knee. "I love you more than anything in the world, Megan."

Her world tipped on its axis. This couldn't be happening. It had to be a dream or a hallucination.

She reached out, touching his chest, feeling his heartbeat, confirming he was real. Then she drew in a shuddering breath, and tears formed at the corners of her eyes.

He caught her hand and held it against his chest. "Will you marry me?"

She stared at the huge ring in amazement, trying to

quantify what was happening, trying to decide whether to laugh or cry or shout with joy.

Collin had come back. He'd said he loved her. He'd brought her a blender drink and surprised her with a diamond. And *what* a diamond!

"Well?" he prompted.

"I didn't know they made them that big," was the first jumbled thought to make it out of her brain.

He tilted the ring box back so that he could gaze at the stone. "I know what a high value you place on expensive jewelry," he deadpanned.

Megan felt her face flush with embarrassment.

"My plan," he said, "was that even if you didn't particularly want me, you'd really want the ring."

She groaned and covered her face with her hands.

"Hey." Collin tipped her chin back up. "You know I'm only joking."

"I don't need a ring like that."

"But I want you to have a ring like that. You said it yourself—diamonds show a certain commitment to a relationship. And I'm feeling just about as committed as it gets."

She reached out to touch the beautiful stone, wondering how she could have possibly gotten so lucky.

"I'd have bought you a bigger one if I didn't think it would be hard to lift your hand," he said.

"It's absolutely gorgeous."

"Can I take that as a yes?"

Megan looked up into Collin's eyes. "Yes." She wrapped her arms around his neck. "Definitely yes. I love you, Collin."

He hugged her close, a teasing note in his voice. "I knew the ring would work."

She bopped him one on the shoulder.

"By the way," he whispered, kissing her cheek, her temple, the edge of her ear, "just so we're clear—I *love* you in sweatpants."

Then he slipped his hands down her body to hook his thumbs into her elastic waistband. "Of course, I love you out of them, too."

temperature
rising!

PLAYING GAMES by Dianne Drake
On air she's the sexy, sassy radio shrink – off air she's
mild-mannered Roxy Rose. Both have only one desire –
the sexy handyman next door.

UNDERCOVER WITH THE MOB
by Elizabeth Bevarly
Jack Miller isn't the type you bring home to mum,
which is exactly why Natalie should stay clear of him.
But her attraction to him is undeniable, as is her need
to uncover his story.

WHAT PHOEBE WANTS by Cindi Myers
Men think Phoebe is a pushover, but now she's refusing to take
orders from anyone – especially hunky Jeff Fisher. Because
now it's all about what Phoebe wants.

On sale 2nd June 2006

*Available at WHSmith, Tesco, ASDA, Borders, Eason, Sainsbury's
and all good paperback bookshops*

www.millsandboon.co.uk